I Love Me More...

By
D.C. Williams

Michelle

After years of trying to save her marriage, an unexpected phone call forces her to acknowledge what she's tried to ignore – a definite change is needed in her life, starting with learning to love herself first.

Ronnie

Feeling like he was forced into marriage by an unplanned pregnancy, he quickly finds out that the grass really isn't greener on the other side when his wife files for divorce and he's left alone. Realizing that he wants her back, what is he willing to do to prove that he's worthy of her love again?

This is a revised version of the original

I Love Me More is a sequel to His Choice, Her Decision.

Please share your thoughts and comments by emailing me at
dcwilliams3love@gmail.com

To everything there is a season, and a time to every purpose under heaven.
Ecclesiastes 3:1

Prologue

1 year later...

Ronnie and I are headed to his parent's house for their annual 4th of July celebration. Funny thing is, for us, it's not much of a celebration. After Sharon and Aiden's wedding nine months ago, we decided to try marriage counseling for a second time, which was his idea. I'm still trying to figure out how he expected for our marriage to be saved with him still continuing to cheat? Needless to say, I met with my attorney on this past Tuesday to file for the divorce that I should have filed for when we returned home from the Bahamas last summer.

"Michelle, we're almost there. For my parent's sake, could you please *try* and act like you're happy?"

Continuing to stare out the car window, I'm only attending this little get together so that I can spend some time with Rhonda and Sharon. We've gotten really close since our vacation and they've both promised that no matter what happens with me and Ronnie, we're going to keep in contact with each other.

"Oh believe me, I'm trying really hard not to go in there and tell everybody what a lying ass cheat you are. But for your parent's sake, I won't."

Rubbing the back of his head, he glances in my direction, "look Michelle, I'm sorry. I know I messed up and I promise you..."

Holding my hand up, "save it, I don't even care anymore. Just get us there so that we can get this over with."

Releasing a heavy sigh, "I really appreciate you for agreeing to come with me." He says. "I'm not ready to have to explain our divorce to my parent's yet. My mom is going to be devastated when she finds out that I've ruined my marriage."

Still staring out the window, to avoid looking at him, "just remember, I'm not doing this for you."

He's more concerned about his mom than he is about me. It's always been like that. Often, I'm reminded that falling for Ronnie was a big mistake. When we were in college, I felt like he was the most positive person in my life, besides my best friend, Yolanda, and I didn't want to lose him. I realize that getting pregnant to try and trap him wasn't the smartest thing to do, but learning that the man who I put on such a high pedestal is no different from any other, really hurts.

Pulling up in front of the Wen's home, Sharon and Aiden have also just arrived and are getting their babies out of their SUV. Aiden is carrying Maddison, a real daddy's girl, while Jaxson is holding onto Sharon's hand as she's walking in our direction.

"Hey Michelle, I was wondering if you'd made it here already." She says. Giving each other a hug, I hear Ronnie mumbling something under his breath as he's getting out of the car.

"Sis, you don't see me standing here?"

"Yeah, I see you." She snidely responds. "Anyways, Michelle. I'm glad you changed your mind and decided to come. You know mom's prepared a feast."

Nodding my head, "I can already taste her beans." I shared the news of our separation with Sharon on yesterday and she knows that I'm in the process of looking for a place to live. Although she didn't say much on the matter, she told me that I had to do what makes me happy.

"Hey guys." Aiden says, waiting by the curb for Sharon to join him. "Seems we're all here."

Clearly, Sharon is mad at him because she walks right past him like he isn't standing there. Smirking at me, he shrugs his shoulder and kisses Maddison on her cheek. Those two are hilarious. They're always arguing about something. Yet, they're madly in love.

"Mom, dad, we're here." Sharon yells, as we're all entering the foyer, heading for the family room. Dad is the first one to greet us. Picking up Jaxson, he gives Sharon and then me a hug. Leaning over to kiss Maddison, she turns her head in the opposite direction, laying it against her daddy's shoulder. "You know how she is daddy, she'll come around when she wants something."

"I know." Mr. Wen says, "Aiden has her spoiled rotten." Kissing Jaxson, "at least you love your granddad, don't you little fella?"

"She's not spoiled." Aiden says, with a slight frown on his face, "she's well loved."

Smiling at Aiden, because that's what he's known to say concerning his babies, we follow Mr. Wen into the family room where his wife, in grandma fashion, takes Maddison away from her daddy and showers her with kisses. She's resistant at first, but eventually, she gives in with belly giggles.

Rhonda, Michael and their three children along with Camille and SJ are sitting in front of the flat screen television watching Sean and Sebastian battle against each other in a game of Madden. Taking a seat next to Camille, I really love this family and I'm going to miss them. But, I love me more!

Chapter One

Today's the big day. I'm finally moving out of the house that I've shared with Ronnie for the past four years. Sitting on my bed, or rather Ronnie's bed now, since he's keeping the house, I think back to when we first met. It was during my freshman year of college at the University of San Diego.

I was attending on a full academic scholarship, while working in the student hall for extra money. Having little to no support from my family, I had no choice but to work hard if I wanted to make something of myself. On the particular day that we met, I was really considering giving up. I had just gotten off the phone with my mother who had called to ask me for money to pay her phone bill. Knowing that I was barely getting by, she still had the nerve to try and put me down for saying no. *"You think you better than me and your brother's cause you in college? You wouldn't even be there if it wasn't for me and don't you forget it. Don't think you better than us cause you not!"* That was then and this is now and it's still the same conversation. Anyways, I was sitting in the library staring at my book. Realizing that I was too upset to focus, I decided to head back to my apartment to try and study. Getting up from my chair, I bumped into Ronnie. He was so fine, I literally felt like I was going to pass out.

"Sorry, I didn't see you."

Smiling at me with his brow raised, "it's okay, are you alright?"

"I, I'm okay." I responded, stuttering like a fool because he was absolutely gorgeous! He stood about 6'4" tall, smooth caramel skin and perfect white teeth. He was fine! Moving to get around him, "um, excuse me and again, I'm really sorry."

"Hey, you don't have to apologize. Are you leaving?"

"Uh, yeah." I respond, glancing up at him.

"Too bad. I was going to ask if you wanted to study together."

Looking around as if contemplating his invitation, "no, I've got to go. Maybe another time."

Walking away, I heard him call out, "by the way, my name is Ronnie."

Getting up from the bed, those were the good ole days. At the time, I thought he was my savior sent by God to show me the positive side of life and to help me get through college. Now, I know for a fact that he was no savior at all, just a source of motivation to keep me going. Yep, six years is too long to have put myself through hell being married to a man who only cared about me when things were going his way. It's definitely time to move on.

Chapter Two

Michelle is moving out of the house today, so I decided to come and hang out at my brother, Sean's. Normally, I work from home on Friday's, but I didn't want to stick around and watch her walk out of my life knowing damn well that with the way that I've treated her, I have no right to ask her to stay.

For the past few days, she hasn't said much at all to me. Really no different than it's been for the past few weeks. She does her thing and I do mine. For some odd reason, the finality of it all is really bothering me. I really messed up.

Lying back on Sean's sofa with the television volume barely audible, I close my eyes while blowing out a deep breath. I remember the first time I saw Michelle in the student library. She was getting up from her chair and bumped into me. Instead of getting annoyed at her for being clumsy, I was caught in a trance. At 5'5", she was so beautiful. She had her long, thick hair pulled back into a low ponytail and was wearing a fitted tee shirt with a pair of blue jean shorts that showed off her creamy brown skin. She kept apologizing and all I could imagine doing was pulling her into my arms to see if her lips tasted as good as they looked.

Michelle was different. She was so innocent and basically idolized me back then. I think that's what made it so easy for me to cheat on her. Every man likes a whore in one aspect and a lady in the other. Michelle was my lady. I respected her too much to do some of the things that I liked to do with other girls.

It took me almost two months to even get a conversation from her. She was so isolated and always working hard to prove herself. I later found out that the force behind her work ethic was so she wouldn't end up like her freeloading mother and sorry ass brothers. Most of our problems have been because of them. Always asking for money. Always thinking that Michelle owes them something. No wonder her dad left their sorry asses. The last straw came sometime last year when her mom had the nerve to ask me to co-sign for a car for her son to get back and forth to work. I couldn't believe it. And what ticked me off even more was Michelle acting like she didn't know that they had asked. I was so damned pissed that I hooked back up with Felecia. Big mistake!

I met Felecia one weekend while my sister, Rhonda, was home from college. She was always bringing her friend's home with her when she visited. I was seventeen at the time, and as soon as I saw her getting out of Rhonda's car, I knew she was a freak by the way she was chewing her gum. On that particular weekend, my parents were having a gathering at our house and the place was crowded. I was sitting at the desk in my room listening to the radio when she walked in and locked the door. I was so damn nervous I didn't know what to do. I remember her asking me if I liked her and all I could do was nod. Dropping to her knees in between my legs, she started rubbing my penis while tonguing the hell out of me. I had never been kissed like that by any girls my age and then she did it, she gave me a blow job. Blew. My. Damn. Mind! She didn't even have to tell me not to say anything because it was our little secret. Every time Rhonda came home from that day forward, it was a given that Felecia was going to be with her. I think the excitement in our relationship was that I was sneaking around and having mad sex with an older woman. She was my teacher and that freak taught me well.

Even when I met and married Michelle, we continued to fool around off and on. But for some reason, this last time was different with Felecia. Normally, she's had a man in her life, so we both knew that it was just about the sex. Next thing I know, I'm lying to my wife to go be with her ass. Shit backfired in my face when the bitch started being all clingy and called Michelle, giving her blow by blow details of our relationship and a copy of the lease to her apartment with my name signed on the dotted line. Damn, I messed up!

Getting up from the sofa, I walk out onto the balcony to stare down at the beach. I've never really cared about Felecia beyond sex. She was just something to do. I'll never forget the look on Michelle's face when she confronted me. I thought for sure I was going to get away with my lie until she threw that damn lease down on the bed. If I could have strangled Felecia and not gone to jail that day, I would have. And all that trifling skank had to say after all I've done for her ass was, "*I got tired of playing second fiddle to your wife.*"

Got tired of playing second fiddle to my wife? A wife who I haven't slept with in the past three months. A wife who can't stand the sight of me. A wife who loved me so much that she got pregnant her senior year of college to keep me from breaking up with her. A wife who lost my baby because of the stress I caused her. A wife who got so tired of my shit that she filed for divorce. A wife who told her attorney that she didn't want anything, but her freedom. A wife who at this exact moment is moving out of the home that we both worked hard to purchase. Rubbing my hands down my face, what is wrong with me? How did I manage to lose the one woman who I truly love, but had a piss poor way of showing her? I need to see her before she leaves.

Chapter Three

"Michelle, I think that's the last of the boxes."

Coming down the stairs, after one final sweep to make sure that I have everything, "thank you, Tommy."

Tommy is a friend of my stepbrother, Zeke. When my step-mother found out that I had filed for a divorce and was moving, she called him to see if he could help. Since Tommy owns a moving company, Zeke solicited his services.

"It looks like I have everything, so I'm ready if you are."

Holding out his hand, "lead the way gorgeous."

"Gorgeous?" Tommy and I both turn to the sound of the voice coming from the kitchen. "Michelle, you're still a married woman. I don't appreciate being disrespected in my home."

Looking at Ronnie like he's lost his damned mind. "Excuse me, what are you talking about?" Not wanting Tommy to get caught in the middle of his foolishness, "whatever Ronnie, no one is disrespecting your home, we're leaving."

Staring at Tommy in an effort to try and intimidate him, something he's good at, "you think I could talk to you for a minute?"

"Nope. We're leaving."

Walking to the door ahead of Tommy, he reaches around him to grab my left arm. Feeling Tommy's hand on the small of my back, I know that Ronnie is only trying to start a fight and I don't want Tommy or Zeke in my business any more than they already are. Turning, "Um, Tommy, you can head on over to the apartment. This won't take long." Handing him my key, Ronnie is fuming.

Taking the key from me, Tommy has his eyes set on Ronnie as well. "You sure about that baby girl?"

"I'm sure. I'll be right behind you." Nodding at me, he reluctantly leaves.

Still gripping my arm, "what in the hell was that? I guess he's my replacement, huh? Is that who you've been screwing?"

"What! What do you want Ronnie?"

Still gripping my arm, "why was he touching you like that?"

"Let go of my arm." I'm saying, trying to pull away from him. "It's none of your business how he or anyone else touches me."

Still gripping my arm, he's glaring at me, "is that right?"

Trying to pry his hand from my arm, "yeah, that's right. Now let go of my arm!"

"Why did you give him a key to your apartment?"

"Ronnie, let go of my arm." Tightening his grip. "He's a mover. I know you don't think much of me, but I think more of myself than to get involved with Tommy. He's married."

"He sure as hell wasn't touching you like he's a married."

"Well, if anyone knows how a married man touches someone other than his wife, it would be you. Right?"

"Don't start, okay? I need to talk to you."

Frowning at him, "could you please let go of my arm?"

Staring at me, I'm not sure what I see. Regret? Surely not. He's never cared much how he's treated me. Every gift purchased, was out of guilt. He was my first love and he used that to his advantage. If he cared, then being faithful shouldn't have been a problem for him.

Releasing my arm, "you know Michelle, I don't know what to say to you that will make a difference at this point. I want you to know that I love you and maybe, I just wasn't ready to get married." Pausing, "I mean, we were much younger then and had you not gotten pregnant, maybe things would have worked out for us."

Closing my eyes, I shake my head. "Ronnie, you don't have to say anything. It is what it is. I think I've grown and I've learned from this experience. Now, it's time to move on." Taking the house key off of my key ring, I place it in his hand. "Take care of yourself."

Turning to leave, he grabs me from behind. Wrapping his arms around my waist, he kisses the side of my neck, "Michelle..."

Taking a deep breath, I feel absolutely nothing. I've allowed this man with his beautiful caramel skin and slanted eyes, compliments of his Asian father, to walk all over me for over six years, but no more. I'm making a new start in my life. I'm twenty seven years old and it's time for me to let go of the excess luggage that my mother, my brothers and Ronnie have plagued me with. Learning to love me was a long process and I refuse to go backwards.

"Ronnie, I really need to go. Is that all you had to say?"

Still holding on, he places his hands flat on my stomach. I can feel his erection pressing against my back, but I'm so not going there. Three months ago, after finding out that he had cheated again with Rhonda's friend, I decided that I'm not going to jeopardize my health and risk getting a sexually transmitted disease from him. Even after he swore that he used protection, I wasn't convinced then and I'm still not convinced that he protected himself.

Placing my hands on top of his to remove them, "Ronnie, Tommy's waiting for me. I need to go." Hesitating, "look, maybe we can talk later." I knew it was a lie the moment it left my lips.

Finally, he releases his hold and steps back. "You've changed. I have a feeling that once you walk out of this house, the chances that you'll ever speak to me again are slim to none." Opening the door for me, "Michelle...." he says, clearing his throat, "take care of yourself."

I can't believe I don't feel anything for him anymore. I've actually been somewhat nervous about today's move. Not knowing how I would feel walking away from the home that I've poured all my love into, hoping that I could save my marriage which in all realness, was doomed from day one. Ironically, all I feel is peace.

Chapter Four

Reaching over to beat the hell out of my clock, my head is pounding. I've had this damn headache going on two days now. Normally, Michelle is the first one up, so I never even hear the alarm going off at six in the morning. Normally, I hear the shower. Normally, I wake up with an erection the size of Texas knowing that my fine ass wife is in the next room pampering herself for a new day.

Sitting up in bed, laughing to myself, who the hell am I kidding? Yeah, I woke up with an erection the size of Texas, but for the past three months my wife refused to take care of anything pertaining to me. *"Get the hell away from me. I'm not taking care of anything. Call Felecia, I'm sure she'll be more than happy to take care of your trifling, cheating ass!"*

Leaning against the headboard, I slide my hand down inside my boxers to embrace my buddy. The only action he's been getting lately is hand action. And to be honest, if I can't get satisfaction from my wife, I don't want it from anyone else. Especially, not from Felecia.

That bitch actually thought that when my wife found out about us that I would continue to see her ass. Not only did I break it off with her, I threw her ass out on the streets. I had no problems paying the re-letting fee to that apartment complex after what she did.

I never thought I would miss Michelle this much, but I do. I miss making love to her in the mornings before going to work. I miss hearing her moan when she's having an orgasm. And I really miss that giggling sound she used to make whenever I would tease one of her many sensitive spots.

Too bad I was too stupid to realize that when I had her. Getting up from bed, this is day one.

Chapter Five

Five more minutes. I need five more minutes. Reaching over to press the snooze button on my alarm clock, I'm completely exhausted. I stayed up way too late last night watching movies. I never knew that being single could be so wonderful! This is the first time in my twenty seven years that I've lived alone, and I love it! All through college, I lived with my best friend, Yolanda, and from there I've been with Ronnie, so this is totally new for me.

Turning over in bed, I can't even contain the smile on my face, I feel so free. No more worrying about Ronnie, my mother or my brothers. It's all about me.

On Saturday, Tommy kept telling me that he has the perfect guy for me to meet. According to Tommy, his friend Malcolm, is thirty five years old and has his own computer software business here in San Diego. As good as he sounds, I'm not ready to start dating again. If there's one thing that I learned from being with Ronnie, it's that I can be selfish without apology.

Thinking of Ronnie, I still can't believe his sorry ass attempt at an apology on Saturday. Funny how bold he was over a year ago when he announced that he wanted a divorce just prior to his parent's anniversary/family vacation. *"I'm sick of being married to you and having to take care of your ghetto ass family."* He had no idea that I knew each and every time that he started with that crap that he was cheating with Felecia. He thought because I never complained about him staying out late, leaving early or not coming home at all that I was oblivious to what was going on. The idiot had no idea that his skank was going to call and blow his cover. I'll never forget that phone call...

I had just made it home from work and was about to take a shower when the home phone rang. Usually, the only people who called our home phone was either telemarketers or my family. Assuming that it was my family, due to the time, I answered without looking at the caller id. Leaning against the kitchen counter to brace myself for what I knew was going to be drama, *"hello."*

"Yes, can I speak to Ronald?"

Ronald? No one calls Ronnie by his legal name. *"Sorry, Ronnie's not home."*

"Is this Michelle?"

Hesitating, *"this is Michelle. May I ask whose calling?"*

"This is Felecia. Ronald's girlfriend."

His girlfriend? Humph! His side hoe is more appropriate. Shaking my head, *"Ronnie's not here, but I'll tell him that you called."*

"Girl, are you for real? I just told you that your husband is cheating on your ass and all you can say is that you'll let him know I called?"

Are you for real is the question. *"I'm honestly not sure how I'm supposed to respond, Felecia. It's not every day that my husband's girlfriend calls my house asking to speak to him so, if you're expecting for me to get upset, it's not happening."*

Laughing into the phone, *"I guess that's why Ronnie cheats on your gullible ass. Anyway, I didn't call for him. I was actually calling to talk to you."*

This bitch is crazy! *"Talk to me about what?"*

"About your divorce. He told me that he filed over six months ago and I know it don't take six months to get a divorce so I need to know what's the hold up?"

"Hold up of what?" Yeah, this bitch is crazy all right.

"The divorce. I need to know how much longer it's going to take for it to be finalized. He told me just the other night that he's tired of taking care of you and your ghetto ass family and he wants out."

Laughing to myself, *"is that what he told you?"*

"Yeah, that's what he told me and like I said, I'm tired of waiting. He thinks that because he pays my rent that I'm going to wait around for his ass to make a move. It don't get that good. Baby please, the dick is good, but if he thinks paying my rent is going to keep me…"

Just as I'm about to hang up on this lunatic…wait, did she just say that he's paying her rent? Cutting her off in midsentence, *"excuse me, did you say he's paying your rent?"*

Sounding all triumphant like she's accomplished her goal, *"yes, that's exactly what I said. I'm surprised you haven't noticed all the money missing from your account because he takes real good care of me."*

I'll bet his cheating ass does. *"Listen Felecia, I'm not sure why you're calling me. Sounds to me like you need to talk to Ronnie. As for the divorce, you won't have to wait much longer because I'm going to be taking care of that real soon."* The moment the words left my lips, I knew without a doubt that that's exactly what I'm going to do. I don't deserve this from him or anyone else.

Silence. Finally, clearing her throat, *"doesn't it bother you that your husband is never home? That he's always spending time with me?"*

Hell no! *"No, it doesn't bother me because I'm never home either. But, I'll bet Ronald neglected to tell you that. Didn't he?"*

"Girl please. Ronnie said that you're always nagging at him for not being home and that you've been begging him for years not to leave you."

Lying bastard! *"Wow! I can't believe he told you that. I see I'm not the only one your boyfriend's been lying to."*

Silence. *"You know Michelle, I don't get you. Here I call to tell you that the man you're married to is taking care of me and you haven't raised your voice or yelled one time. You knew about me before you got married and yet, you still married him."* Laughing into the phone, *"but then again, Ronald did say that you're very passive and naive."*

Seems like Ronald has said a lot about me. Still, I don't owe her anything. *"I choose what's important to get upset over and Ronnie's cheating with you isn't important to me, so I'm sorry if you're not getting the reaction that you were expecting. However, I think it's pathetic for a woman your age to even be calling me with crap like this. That's what I don't get about you. Because even though he's been screwing around with you, he married me. If I'm passive and naïve, what does that make you? Desperate?"*

Silence. A sure sign of defeat. *"You wouldn't be so calm unless you think I'm lying. I have proof. His name is signed on the dotted line of the lease to my apartment."* Laughing, *"I can show you the lease honey."*

Honey? This tramp can't be serious. I'm about to say that I don't need her to show me a damn thing, but this proof will most likely work in my favor when I file for my divorce. *"I believe you and if it's not too much trouble, could you email me a copy of your lease to help expedite our little situation?"*

Sounding all excited again, *"I sure can. Give me your email address."*

Giving her my email info, I hung up the phone. For the strangest reason, I was glad for Felecia's call. It was just what I needed to make a change and get rid of the excess weight of unhappiness in my life that involved Ronnie, my mother and my two brothers.

Knowing that I didn't want to have to deal with Ronnie when he got home, I packed an overnight bag and decided to spend the night at a hotel.

The next morning, I printed off the email that Felecia sent containing a copy of the lease, signed by Ronnie, along with some other receipts and her bank statement showing how well he's been taking care of her and met with an attorney.

I'd been avoiding Ronnie's calls from that night and the next morning because I had absolutely nothing to say to him.

Pulling into the garage, I barely had the door open before Ronnie was all up in my face talking about, *"where the hell have you been?"*

Walking past him to go inside the house, he was literally on my heels. Entering our bedroom, I placed my purse on the bed and headed straight for the closet to grab a pair of jeans and tee shirt.

"Michelle, where the hell have you been?" He says, *enunciating each word.*

"Out."

"I know you've been out!" He yells. *"Where were you and why weren't you answering your phone? Let me find out you been messing around and so help me God..."*

Staring at this fool, he's so full of shit. *"Well, let's see, after I hung up from talking to your girlfriend on yesterday, I left, checked into a hotel and oh yeah, I met with an attorney to file for the divorce that she thinks you filed for six months ago because according to her, even though the dick is good, she's tired of waiting on your ass."*

"My what? I don't know what you're talking about. And why would you be meeting with an attorney without first discussing it with me?"

Turning to face him, *"You don't know what I'm talking about? Really? Well from what I was told, you're tired of taking care of me and my ghetto ass family."*

"What? Who told you that? That's some bullshit and you know it."

Staring at him, *"you've never said that?"*

"I...like I said it's bullshit and unless you can tell me who said it..."

"Your girlfriend told me you said it."

Trying to pass him to go back into the bedroom, he's standing in the doorway, not bulging.

"I don't know what you're talking about."

"Sure, you don't."

Finally, moving just enough for me to get past him, *"like I said, I don't know what you're talking about."*

Sitting down on the bed, *"so you didn't tell Felecia that you filed for a divorce six months ago?"*

Pacing back and forth in front of me, not saying anything. His normal tactic when he's trying to manipulate a situation to make it my fault, he stops and stares at me. Reaching into my purse, I pull out a copy of the email. Throwing it down on the bed, I move past him to go into the bathroom, locking the door behind me.

Turning on the shower, I want to kick myself for being so blinded by Ronnie. Trying to trap him was just plain dumb on my part. I should have listened to Yolanda. At the time, I felt like I couldn't live without him. When he started avoiding me and making excuses for never being available, I knew he was seeing someone else. Then one night, he came to my apartment and said that we needed to talk. Knowing that he was going to break up with me, I told him I was finally ready to have sex. I was a virgin at the time and felt that if I finally gave him what he wanted, that he wouldn't want anyone but me. Wrong! When he found out that I wasn't taking the birth control pills that he had gone to the campus clinic with me to get, he was pissed and I was pregnant.

Banging on the door. "Michelle, open up. We need to talk. I can explain this."

Turning off the water, how can he explain his signature on another woman's lease? Drying off and getting dressed, I pull my hair back into a ponytail. Opening the door, he's standing by the bed with the email in his hand staring at me.

"How did you get this?" He's asking, voice is just above a whisper.

"I already told you where I got it from."

Coming to stand in front of me, *"did Felecia give you this?"*

Walking around him to go back into the closet to grab a pair of sandals, *"who else would have given me the lease Ronnie? My question to you is this, if you wanted to be with her, then why prolong the inevitable? I'm not begging you to stay with me anymore. If you'll recall, I haven't for a while."*

Not saying anything is a clear sign that Ronnie is guilty as sin. *"Why were you on the phone talking to her anyway? You should have known that she was trying to start some shit."*

Holding onto one of my shoes, I have a sudden urge to knock the hell of him. Following my instinct, my shoe somehow flies out of my hand and hits him in the head. *"Don't try and reverse this on me you sorry piece of shit! You've been cheating and your ass is caught."*

"Michelle, don't hit me again! That skank don't mean shit to me. If I wanted to divorce your ass, I would have done so a long time ago instead of going to marriage counselling."

Is he serious? Throwing my other shoe at him, "you are so full of shit!"

Charging towards me, "didn't I just tell you not to hit me? And over some trifling bitch!"

All in my face, we're yelling at each other. "She's not too trifling, you're paying her rent!"

"I was helping that ho out because she was having financial problems!"

"Who in the hell do you think you're talking to Ronnie? Did you're helping her out mean that you had to tell her about my family?"

"Don't be ridiculous, everybody knows your family is ghetto as hell. That's not new news!"

"I'm sick of you, Ronnie! I'm sick of you putting my family down! I'm sick of you mistreating me! And, I'm sick of you cheating on me!" Pushing him, he grabs my right arm.

"Don't make me hurt you, Michelle. I already told you the deal."

"Well here's my deal, I'm divorcing your ass!" I feel so good. I've never stood up for myself with him. Not like this anyway.

Pointing his finger in my face, "you know what Michelle? You're stupid! I can't believe that you would let some trick call here and fill your head with lies but if this is what you want, then you've got it. I'm tired of arguing with you over this shit."

Slapping his hand out of my face while he's still holding onto my arm, "no Ronnie, you're the one who's stupid. Is that not your name signed on her lease?"

"What in the hell is wrong with you girl? Since when do you feel the need to hit me? Do you know how bad I could hurt you if I really wanted to?"

Tears streaming down my face, he has no idea. "You know what Ronnie, for the past six years I've allowed you to walk all over me. Listened to you complain about how I ruined your life by getting pregnant when the truth of the matter is, you ruined my life. You would have done better by walking away when I told you that I was pregnant because as we can see, the baby didn't live and we could have both gone our separate ways. And just so you know, you've caused me so much emotional pain that the physical probably wouldn't even phase me."

Letting go of my arm, he stands there just staring at me not saying anything. Retrieving my shoes, I grab my purse and leave the house.

I thank God for that phone call. What was meant to hurt me only pushed me to do what I should have done years ago.

Finally getting out of bed, it's time to face the work week as Ms. Michelle Barnett.

Chapter Six
11 months later.....

"Hey man, I'm glad you made it." Aiden says, answering the door. "You just missed your sister."

This weekend, I decided to come hang out with the guys here in Bakersfield to take a break from work. Since my divorce, it seems all I do is work.

"Sean and Sebastian are down in the cave watching the game." Aiden says, "you can head on down. I'm going to grab a couple more beers from the kitchen."

"Alright man." Entering Aiden's cave, "what's up fellas?"

"Hey big bro, you finally made it." Sean says, getting up to give me a man's hug.

"What's up, Ronnie?" Sebastian says. "Man, it's been a minute."

"I know, man." I respond, taking a seat on the sofa. "I've been keeping busy with work."

"Hear you there." He says.

When Aiden returns with the beers, he and Sebastian resume whatever conversation they were having before I arrived, while Sean is texting and I'm sitting here pretending to be interested in this boring ass basketball game. After a few minutes, I can feel Sean staring at me. "What?

"Nothing."

"What? You staring at me like you want to say something."

Chuckling, "nothing." He says, shaking his head.

"Man, what is it?"

Smirking, he leans back against the sofa. "You know Michelle is here this weekend, hanging out with the ladies. I saw her earlier today."

"What?" Glancing around the room, Aiden and Sebastian have all of a sudden gotten quiet. Aiden is staring at the television while Sebastian is looking at his phone. "So y'all knew Michelle was here and not once did either of you mention anything about it? That's foul."

Aiden is the first to speak. "Look man, you're my brother and all, but me and your sister are getting along really good right now and I don't want any problems."

"What are you talking about? What problems? It's not even like that. You could have at least told me that she was here."

"And looking good as hell!" Sean says. "I can't believe she cut off all that hair. What is it with women cutting their hair?"

"She cut her hair? I loved her hair." Michelle has the most beautiful hair. Long, thick and healthy.

"Seriously?" Sean says, with his face all scrunched up and shit, "man, you should have thought about her hair when you were paying the beweavable woman's rent."

Laughing at Sean, "home girl does wear a lot of weave." Sebastian says.

Frowning at these fools, "Sean, shut the hell up. You're always trying to stir up some shit. Anyways, where is Michelle?" Once again, Aiden and Sebastian have lost their voices.

Leave it to Sean, "I don't know where she is right now, but we're all going to Capone's tonight and..."

"Sean. Man, stop." Aiden says. "Listen Ronnie, you can't go. If Sharon even thinks I told you about Michelle being here and you show up at that club, she's going to be pissed."

"Aiden, you've turned into such a bitch. If I'm here, do they honestly think I'm not going to be with you guys?"

"Look Ronnie, Aiden is right. You can't go."

"Man, you can go!" Sean says. "And Sebastian, we all know who's wearing the panties in your house. You can't even take a piss without asking Camille's permission."

At that remark, we all laugh "Oh, I'm going. Hold up, is Rhonda here?"

"Nah man, she couldn't make it." Sean says. "Sharon mentioned something about Michael Jr. not feeling well."

Good. The last thing I need is Rhonda staring daggers at me. She's still pissed that I was screwing around with Felecia for all those years. I've always known that Rhonda had a mean streak, but when she found out about what I did, her ass went crazy! Hell, I'm mad at me for screwing around with that stupid ass girl.

Chapter Seven

I'm here in Bakersfield visiting with Sharon and Camille for the weekend. Having not seen them in a while, we made plans for me to come here from Dallas, where I've been for the past few days, attending a business meeting, for some much needed girl time.

We met earlier today for massages at Sharon and Camille's day spa followed by shopping before I had to come back here to the hotel to take part in a conference call to discuss my meeting in Hong Kong on Tuesday. Tonight, we're going out to this club called Capone's.

Since the call ran over, I called Sharon and told her that I'd meet them at the club instead of at her house like we originally planned.

Arriving at the club, I'm texting Sharon to let her know that I'm waiting for her at the entrance. Checking out my surroundings, I see Camille maneuvering through the crowd with Sharon right behind her. "Hey girl," she says, giving me a hug. "I like those pants, you're going to be turning heads in that outfit." I'm wearing patterned, multi-colored earth tone fitted ankle pants, a cream colored, long sleeved sheer blouse with matching camisole and a pair of nude pointed toe pumps.

"Speaking of turning heads, Ronnie's here."

Ronnie's here. Why is he here? "Here at the club?"

"Unfortunately, yes." Sharon says, grabbing my hand. "You know we can go somewhere else, just us girls, if you'd like."

I really don't care. If anything, he's probably the one who's going to be uncomfortable. "No, we can stay here. I'm fine."

Wrapping her arm around my shoulders, "cool, let's go party!" Camille says.

Approaching the bar, everyone, with the exception of Ronnie, is speaking to me. Taking a seat next to Sean, he leans up against my arm, "girl, you look good. I still can't believe you cut off all that beautiful hair." Looking over at Ronnie, "I'm not going to say who, but somebody at this table loved all that hair. At least he said so earlier today."

Rubbing my hand down the back of my short cropped haircut and ignoring Sean's comment, "I hear that a lot." After my divorce was final, I wanted a new look. Cutting my hair was a drastic move, considering how long it was, but I don't have any regrets about my decision. That and taking back my maiden name was key in my new transformation.

The music is popping in here and the dance floor is crowded. A song by DMX comes on and both Sharon and Camille grab me by the hand heading to the dance floor while the guys are moving to a table that just became available. Feeling Ronnie's eyes on me the entire time, I choose to continue to ignore him. This DJ is awesome because he's got one good song after another playing. Then, from out of nowhere, this guy starts dancing with me. At first, it was a touch here and there. Now, he's getting really aggressive. "Could you back up?"

"My bad. Girl, you fine as hell!"

Glancing over at Sharon, she's cracking up laughing. "Michelle, look at Ronnie. He looks like he's about to blow a gasket. You ought to let him touch your ass to see what he does."

I'm not going to respond because I honestly don't care about Ronnie or how he feels. Aside from that, I don't want this guy touching me and I'm tired of dancing. I should have followed Camille off the dance floor twenty minutes ago. Thank God, this song has come to an end so that I can make my exit. "Sharon, I'm going to the restroom."

"I'll go with you. I don't know how much longer Aiden is going to watch me without acting a fool. I could see him over there mentally measuring how close that guy was dancing up on me."

Laughing at Sharon's comment, as we're walking in the direction of the ladies room, "yeah, I'm not trying to get kicked out of this club tonight."

"Right, everybody knows how crazy he gets." She says, standing in line behind me waiting. "Have you talked to Ronnie since your divorce?"

"No." Clearing my throat, "there's nothing for us to talk about."

"You know he put Felecia out of that apartment."

Taking a deep breath, "Sharon, why are you talking to me about Ronnie?"

Shrugging her shoulders, "I don't know...I guess I see something different in him." Giving a half laugh, "Michelle, people can change. Look at Aiden. If he can change, anybody can change."

I know she's only looking out for her brother. If he's changed, then I'm happy for him.

Touching my arm, "hey, I shouldn't have gone there. We came here to have fun, not to talk about Ronnie. Forget I said anything."

"It's okay, I know you love your brother." Crossing my legs, "this line is moving super slow." I say, to change the subject and avoid any tension between the two of us. Besides, I'm dating Malcolm now. She doesn't know anything about him and I sure don't plan to say anything. What I do in my personal life is my business.

Chapter Eight

I should have followed the sensible side of my brain and listened to Aiden and Sabastian. I didn't do that because I wanted to see Michelle. Judging by her actions, she doesn't feel the same.

Damn, she looks so beautiful. More beautiful than when we were married. That short cut brings out another side of sexy in her, a more mature sexy. I can't stop looking at her and she has, without any effort, managed to act as if I'm not sitting here. I'm in such a trance, I've tuned out everything around me while watching her every move. She could always dance. Too bad that after the whole baby ordeal, I barely took her out. We used to go out dancing all the time when we were in college.

"Man, your ex is wearing the hell out of those pants." Sean says, breaking the silence surrounding our table.

Aiden has his eyes completely fixated on Sharon while she's dancing. I've heard how stupid he can get, but I've never seen him in action. While Sebastian on the other hand is just sitting back watching Camille, as if she's dancing only for him. Makes me wonder if what everyone says about Camille controlling their relationship is true. Looks to me like they bring out the best in each other.

Glaring at Sean to keep from getting up to knock the hell out of him, "you shouldn't even be looking at her like that."

"I'm just saying." Pointing to the dance floor, "and I'm not the only one. Look at that fool out there dancing behind her. His eyes are plastered to her ass."

"And he's too damn close!" Aiden says. "I'm just waiting for this fucker who keeps dancing up behind Sharon to make the wrong move. As soon as he does, I'm going to pounce on his sorry ass."

"Not tonight. I mean it Aiden, not tonight." Sebastian says. "I knew the old Aiden was still in there somewhere. Everybody talking about you've changed. That's bullshit. Your ass is still the same."

"Damn right. I'm with Sean on this." Aiden says, as he's looking back at me. "Divorce or not, I'd kick his ass. Not that I'm looking at your ex, but that son of a bitch has touched her at least two or three times inappropriately. Not to mention, he's too damn close!"

"Man, think about what you just said, she's my ex. I can't go out there acting a fool."

All three men say at the same time, "shit!"

Looking around the table, it would be a waste of time for me to challenge them because I know for a fact that they would be out there in a heartbeat acting fools. Even Sean, who doesn't have a clue what the word commitment means, would be out there acting a nut.

"You looked good out there baby." Sebastian says to Camille, who has returned to the table. Sitting down in his lap, they're slobbering all over each other.

"Damn, get a room. No one wants to hear or see you guys carrying on like that." Aiden says.

Looking in his direction, they both burst out laughing. "Jealous?" Sebastian is asking.

Momentarily taking his eyes away from the dance floor, "no, disgusted."

After a few minutes of everyone talking back and forth, Michelle and Sharon are walking off the dance floor. The guy dancing with Michelle has moved on to someone else, less attractive. Finally, Sharon and Michelle return to the table laughing with Camille about two women fighting over some guy in the ladies room. The guys join in on the laughter when Sharon gives us a demonstration of how the one woman snatched off the other chick's wig. I guess if I wasn't so fixated on Michelle, I could join in on their fun. But shit, she won't even look at me.

"Oh Aiden, that's our song. Can we dance?" Sharon is asking as she's pulling Aiden out of his seat. Since we were kids, *'Love's Holiday'* has been one of her favorite songs. When they get up to leave, the others follow suit, leaving me and Michelle alone at the table.

Clearing my throat, "Michelle, would you…"

"Michelle? Girl, is that you? Felton told me you cut off all your hair. It looks good."

Getting up from her seat to hug this fool, "Todd," she says, smiling at him. "What are you doing in Bakersfield?"

"My wife and I are here visiting her sister."

"Is Brandy here at the club with you?"

"Nah, she's out with the ladies. What about Malcolm, is he here with you?"

"No, he's back in San Diego. I was in Dallas for a meeting and came here to hang out with my friends before heading back home."

"By the way, congratulations on the promotion. Junior partner, huh?"

"Thank you."

"I always knew you had it in you, Michelle." He says, "Brockman and Goldstein are lucky to have you."

"I don't know about that, but thanks."

"Girl, what? You're the first black female junior partner at a firm dominated by white men. I'm proud of you." Laughing, "Felton said you still chant that same speech before your presentations."

"Whatever it takes to succeed. Right?"

"Yeah, I guess you're right because it seems to work for you. Look, I better go and really Michelle, I'm proud of you. Kick ass in Hong Kong."

"Will do."

I'm pissed. She just had this long ass conversation with this fool without even acknowledging me. And who the hell is Malcolm? I'm about to go off on her ass, but everyone is returning from the dance floor.

Getting up from the table, she says that she's leaving. Hugging and kissing everyone goodbye, Sean's ass speaks up first. "Michelle, I'll walk you out to your car."

To hell with that. Grabbing Sean by his arm, "Sean, I'll walk her out."

"Ronnie, it's okay. I valet parked, so I'll be fine."

"Well damn, you do remember my name."

Rolling her eyes at me as she walks ahead. "Whatever, it's not like you were talking to me either." Giving her ticket to the attendant, she's looking straight ahead.

"So, how have you been?"

"Fine."

Staring down at her, "congratulations on the promotion."

"Thanks."

"Were you recently promoted?"

Laughing to herself, "May, of last year."

May? We were still married then. The attendant has arrived with her rental car. "Bye Ronnie, good seeing you again." She says, going around to get into the car while he's holding the door open for her. Driving off, I'm still standing there looking at the tail lights. How in the hell did she get a promotion last year without me knowing anything about it? That's bull! I'm ready to leave. I should be following her ass to find out who the hell this Malcolm guy is and how long she's been seeing him. And if this night can't get any worse, I've got to go back inside this club and listen to Sean's ass because I'm sure he's going to have something to say.

Chapter Nine

"Man, you're up early." I'm saying to Aiden as I walk out to join him on their deck.

"When you have kids, sleeping late isn't an option."

Sitting here, not saying anything, I'm deep in thought. Seeing Michelle on last night only confirmed just how much I miss her. Judging by the way she acted towards me, I don't even know where to begin to get her to have a decent conversation with me. "Aiden, I need to ask you a question and I want your honest answer."

"What's up?"

"When you and my sister were going through hard times in your relationship, how did you get her to stay with you? I mean, you messed up how many times and she never left you."

Nodding his head, "she didn't leave me, but she shut me out." Leaning forward in his seat, "you want an honest answer, right?"

"Yes, I want an honest answer."

"With Sharon, there was never any doubt that I loved her. She knew it. She would always say that she saw the side of me that no one else could see." Sitting back in his seat, "we're talking about Michelle, right?"

Exhaling a deep breath, "yeah, I'm talking about Michelle." Frustrated, "man, she acted like I wasn't even there and then I found out that she's seeing some dude named Malcolm. Hearing that shit messed me up big time."

"She actually told you that she was seeing someone?"

"Nah, while everybody was out on the dance floor, she was talking to some guy she knows and he asked her about him."

"Damn. So she's moved on and you want her back."

Leaning back in the chair with my legs stretched out, "I miss her."

"That's evident. I could tell by the way you kept staring at her. Let me ask you a question though, when did you realize that you love her? I mean, from what I could see when you were married, it looked like you were only tolerating her."

Frowning at his last comment, "what the hell does that mean?"

Seeing my confusion, "what I'm saying is, you never acted like she was number one in your life. At least not from what I could see. For instance, I see the love that Sebastian has for Camille. Sebastian told me even before I realized it that I was in love with Sharon. Actually, I saw more emotion from you on last night than I ever saw when you were married."

"Man, she won't even talk to me. Do you know I found out she got a big promotion while we were still married? She not once mentioned anything about a promotion to me. We weren't that bad off."

Not saying anything for a while. "Let me ask you this, why did you cheat on her with Rhonda's friend?"

"I was seeing Felecia on and off before we got married." Shrugging my shoulders, "once I got married, she was just something extra to do."

"Was she the only one?"

"While we were married, yes."

"Did Michelle know about her before you got caught?"

I thought everyone knew this story. "Michelle said she knew each and every time that I cheated on her, even before we got married."

"So you were messy, which means you really didn't give a damn."

"At first, I did. When were in college, I was able do whatever I wanted. She never questioned me because she was always studying and didn't demand much of my time. Once we got married, I think I just got comfortable doing what I wanted and I didn't consider her feelings."

Aiden is quiet, like he's processing what I've just told him. "It's a bitch when you realize the grass really isn't greener on the other side, isn't it?"

"Hell yes! Man, if I had known then what I know now, I would have treated her so much better." Sitting up straight, "how can I get her to talk to me?"

"What do you want to talk about?"

"Shit if I know. I'd like her to know that I miss her."

"That's not going to be good enough. Especially, now that she's involved with someone else." Running his hand through his hair, "I literally watched this woman ignore you without even trying. That means she's not bitter. On the other hand, it also means that she's not going to give you any of her time unless you know how to play your cards right."

"What about ole dude?"

"What about him?" Moving to the edge of his seat using his hands for extra emphasis, "I was Sharon's first. She saved herself for me. I'm the only man she's ever been with. There are *things* that you can do to use to your advantage."

Looking at him out the corner of my eye, "man, I don't want to hear about you sexing my sister."

"Fine. I still have your sister and you're sitting over there looking all depressed and shit. All I'm saying is this, you should know how to get her to open up to you. You were her first, right?" Nodding my head. "Man, women always have love for the first man to pop that cherry. Especially, if it was good. Shit, use puppy dog eyes. Whatever it takes. The thing is, when she does open up, you need to go white guy style on her."

Arms folded across my chest, I laugh at this fool. "Man, what does white guy style mean?"

"Women talk. Black guys like to lick and split." Sitting back smiling, "white guys, we have a theory called push and hold."

"Push and hold?"

This fool is over here nodding with this crazy ass, lopsided grin. "You put that tongue action on her the right way and she'll be pushing trying to get away all while holding your head in place begging you not to stop. They love that shit!"

"Man, black guys eat pussy too."

"Not like white guys. Anyways, stop being all defensive, I'm trying to tell you how to get your woman back because if Malcolm is hitting that, then you've got some competition. Now when you do it, don't stop until she's had two orgasms back to back or begging you to stop. At that point, she'll agree to almost anything you say because you'll be in her head, screwing with her emotions. It's all about breaking down her defenses and I'm telling you, it works every time."

Leaning back in my chair, "I don't know whether to thank you for your advice or kick your ass for manipulating my sister with sex."

Laughing, "Like I said earlier, I'm still with your sister. She knows she's number one in my life. I don't want anyone else but her." Leaning back in his chair, "and the answer to your question is this, you cheated on her because you could. Michelle was first in the way that you provided for her but in all other aspects, she was second because at the time, you felt trapped."

Processing what Aiden has just said, he's absolutely right. "What do you suggest I do to get her to talk to me?"

"You want to know my way or the right way?"

Laughing, "I think I want to try your way. Wait, I won't end up in jail, will I? You're a star, you can get away with doing crazy shit."

"Star or not, you want your woman back? Now see if Michelle had been my woman, she wouldn't have left me at that club last night. I would have followed her to that hotel and we'd be waking up with a smile on our faces." Leaning over, "and that Malcolm guy would be history. Take the choice away from her. Like today, she's driving back to San Diego, you are too. Why can't you ride back together?"

With my arms folded across my chest, I nod. "I thought about that too. I wish I knew which hotel she's staying at."

"Your sister knows." Pointing his hand in my direction, "just don't be obvious when asking. When she tells you, go to the hotel and find out who her rental is through. Then, you call them saying that you're her husband and tell them to pick up the car because she no longer needs it. When she comes out to get into her car, you be there waiting. It's that simple."

Looking at him, I'm skeptical as hell in going about this his way.

"Yeah, I know this is bold as shit, so expect for her to be pissed." He says, laughing. "But, when she calms down, she'll see that you did something out of the ordinary for her, even if it's really for you."

"Man, I don't know. Michelle seems all reserved and quiet, but she'll go berserk on your ass if pushed. Plus, she's changed a lot. I can tell."

"She's changed how she views things. I think she still loves you. Believe me, if she hated you, we would have all seen it, reserved or not. She's at a peaceful place in her life. I could see it in her eyes."

Nodding at his comment. "Yeah, you're right."

"Now stop disturbing my last remaining moments of peace and go get your woman. Oh, and Ronnie, remember this bit of advice, take care of what you have and not what you can get. These women out here are scandalous as hell. Your woman is different. She deserves the best of you."

Getting up to go into the house, "thanks for the advice."

"Anytime." Leaning back in his seat with his head thrown back facing the sun. "Oh and Ronnie, don't forget to call and tell me what she does when you go white guy on her."

Laughing, "man you are nuts!"

Chapter Ten

Walking into the kitchen, Sharon and the babies are sitting at the table eating breakfast.

"Hey big brother. Are you hungry?"

"Morning sis." Taking the spoon out of Jaxson's hand, "no, I'm good."

Grabbing at the spoon, "stop teasing him Ronnie."

"Stop!" Maddison screams at me. "I tell my daddy on you."

Laughing at her, "I'm not scared of your daddy."

Going back and forth with Maddison, Sharon finally intervenes after laughing at our exchange.

"Ronnie, stop messing with my babies so they can finish their breakfast."

"Your babies are rotten." Taking a seat at the table, "so what do you have planned for today?"

"Not much. "

"You and the girls aren't going to hang out again today?"

"No. Camille and Sebastian have plans today."

"Un-huh, hmm."

Smirking at me, "hmm? That hmm wouldn't have anything to do with Michelle, would it?"

Frowning at her, "why would you ask me that?"

"I saw you staring at her last night."

"I was not staring at her."

Poking her lips out, "stop lying."

"Girl, I'm not lying. I mean, I noticed her. She looked good. But, I wasn't staring at her."

"Okay, Ronnie. Whatever you say. It would be easier if you just admit that you want her back. I saw how you were looking at her and she saw you too."

"Did she say anything?"

Glaring at me with that I knew you were lying look, "no, she didn't say anything. Not about you she didn't."

"You think she's still upset with me? I haven't talked to her since the divorce."

"I don't think so." Wiping food off of Jaxson's face, "to be honest with you, I think she's just moved on. When we told her that you were at the club on last night, she didn't act like it bothered her one way or the other." Placing her hand over her heart, "if that had been me, I would've probably freaked out and left."

"She ignored me the entire time." Damn, did I just say that to my sister?

"Yeah, she did. And when I mentioned to her how you were watching her on the dance floor, she said she didn't want to talk about you." Looking up at me, "Ronnie, you hurt her."

Staring down at my hands, "do you know anything about the guy she's dating?"

"Who told you about Malcolm?"

"Who told you about Malcolm?"

"Don't look at me like that." Pointing at me, "you messed up your marriage. Anyways, I overheard her and Yolanda talking about him on the phone on yesterday while we were at the spa."

Frowning, "I hate Yolanda. I don't know how she can be friends with that skank."

"There's nothing wrong with Yolanda."

"She's a trifling ho. You know she tried to fix Michelle up with some dude while we were in college. That's why I can't stand her ass."

"Yolanda is the female version of you. That's why you don't like her."

Toying with Maddison, "think she's serious about this guy?"

"I don't know Ronnie and why do you care?"

"I miss her. I've missed her. Seeing her on yesterday made me feel like I need... I don't know. I just miss her."

Reaching across the table to grab my hand, she squeezes, "talk to her Ronnie. That's my only advice. We all make mistakes, she knows that." Hesitating, "you know she's driving back to San Diego by herself today. Maybe you could call and ask her if maybe the two of you could share a ride."

Damn, this is easier than I thought. "I know her cell phone number is the same, but I doubt if she'll answer if I call. She hasn't in the past."

"Use our home phone. She'll think it's me."

Contemplating my next move, should I follow Sharon's advice or Aiden's? Looking at Sharon, she seems really happy. Maybe she's, nah, I'm going to follow Aiden's advice. "I don't know. Calling her, she could easily say no. I'd like to see her in person."

Looking out towards the deck, "don't let Aiden get you sent to jail."

Almost unable to contain my laugh, "what? What are you talking about?"

"That's Aiden talk. I know. Anyways, she's staying at The Five Square Hotel and you better not tell her that I told you."

Walking around the table to kiss her on the cheek, "thanks sis. I owe you big time."

"Yeah, whatever. Oh, and she's leaving around ten."

"Thanks. I love you sis."

"Love you too."

Chapter Eleven

I'm so ready for this phone call to end. I know that this is a major account and I'm well aware that our presentation in Hong Kong is crucial, but Felton is working on my last nerve! Not only is he my co-worker, he's also a really good friend and a gifted architect. He's been in Hong Kong since last Wednesday and it seems that the powers that be are trying to make some changes to our original design for building a state of the art housing complex which is causing stress because were almost twenty thousand dollars over the budget that we were given.

"I'm going to email a list of all the changes for you to review prior to your arrival." Hearing him sigh into the phone, "I swear, these guys are some conniving ass bastards. Trying to tell me that this is what they wanted in the very beginning."

"They were the ones who signed off on the original plans. No one forced them. Anyways, at this point it doesn't matter. We need to try to accommodate them so that they won't cancel the contract. Which, I seriously doubt will happen considering they have just as much vested in this project as we do."

"You're probably right. Listen, I'm going to get some sleep. I'm seeing double. Be careful driving home and I'll see you when you get here."

Closing my laptop, "okay, I will. Try not to stress too much." Hanging up the phone, it's almost ten thirty. I planned to be on the road by ten. Finishing up with packing my luggage, I'm headed for the checkout desk. Coming off the elevator, my phone rings. It's Malcolm. Approaching the desk, I reach into my back pocket to hand the attendant the entry card to my room.

"Good morning babe. Just wanted to see if you're on the road."

"Hold on Malcolm." Covering the phone, "good morning, I'm checking out of room 2104."

"Okay. I'll be right with you."

Nodding at the attendant, "no, I'm just now leaving. I got stuck on the phone with Felton."

"Ms. Barnett, will you be charging your visit with us?"

"Yes." Opening my wallet, I pass her my credit card. "Felton is driving me crazy worrying over this account. I've been talking to him off and on since seven."

"It can be difficult having to deal with people from other countries." Malcolm says. "Especially, when money is involved."

Before I can respond, "by the way Ms. Barnett, the rental car company called and said they'll have someone here by noon to pick up the key to your rental car." She says, waiting for my signature.

Puzzled by her statement, "hold on Malcolm, why would the rental car company tell you that? I'm returning the car in San Diego."

Looking nervous, "I'm not sure. I'm just telling you what I was told."

Taking my credit card and receipt from her, "there must be some kind of mistake." Rushing out of the hotel, with my bags in tow, I'm looking for my rental car that's supposed to be parked in front of the hotel. With Malcolm repeatedly asking me what's wrong, it's causing me to panic even more. "The rental car company picked up my car." Letting out a frustrated sigh, "I'll call you back when I get this figured out."

Standing outside, I'm scrolling through my phone looking for their number. "Hi, this is Michelle Barnett and I was just told by the hotel attendant that you picked up my rental car. I need to speak with your manager to find out why the car was picked up and how soon you can get back here with a replacement in like the next ten minutes?"

"Yes, Ms. Barnett. This is Travis, I'm the manager. We received a call from your husband earlier this morning requesting that we pick up the car."

"My husband? I'm not married…" Looking to my left, I see Ronnie approaching with this big ass grin on his face. "Travis, let me call you back."

"Good morning, beautiful."

Glaring at him, "good morning my ass. Did you have the rental car company pick up my car?"

Using his hands to make some moot point, "I was actually expecting a good morning in return, minus the attitude."

Hand on my hip cause I don't have time for his crap, "Ronnie, did you have the rental car company pick up my car?"

"Damn, it's like that?" Holding his hands up in defense, "look, we're both going back to San Diego. I thought we could make the ride together since we haven't talked in a while. I figured it would be a good time for us to catch up on what's been going on with each other."

"We're divorced, that's why we haven't talked in a while!" I'm screaming at him. "I can't believe you would do something like this." Turning my back to him, I'm calling Travis back. "You are such an asshole!"

Laughing at me, "I know damn well you didn't just call me an asshole." Walking up behind me, he grabs the handle to my suitcase and begins to roll it towards his black, Mercedes CL coupe. "Get off the phone and come on."

Walking quickly behind him, "Ronnie, I'm not going anywhere with you. Now give me back my bag!" Finally someone answers the damn phone. "Listen, this is Michelle Barnett." I say, yelling into the phone. "I don't know who in the hell authorized you to take instructions from someone other than the person who rented the car, but you'd better get someone here in like the next ten minutes or I'm suing your asses for breach of privacy!" Ronnie has now placed my suitcase in his trunk and is standing there holding the passenger door open for me with this stupid smirk on his face.

Breaking the few inches of separation between us, he takes, yes, takes my phone out of my hand and turns his back to me, "hello, this is Mr. Wen. I called you this morning to pick up my wife's car. Yes, I'm sorry for the confusion, she doesn't like surprises. Yes, we'll leave the key at the front desk. Yes, still charge the credit card that I gave you this morning." Turning, so that he's facing me, with his hand held out, "give me the key."

Trying not to go off on his ass in front of the few people now standing outside, "give me back my damn phone. Why would you do something like that? I don't have time for your shit today Ronnie."

"The sooner you give me the key, the sooner we can get on the road. I don't have anywhere to be." He says, with a smirk on his face, "I can play this game all day."

"What game? You're the one playing games." Holding out my hand with my eyes narrowed, "give me back my damn phone!"

Grabbing my hand, "Michelle, will you please give me the key? Please. I'm not driving back to San Diego without you sitting beside me so the longer you take, the longer it's going to take for us to leave. Like I said earlier, I have all day. You're the one with the business trip."

I'm so mad, I'm fuming! Handing him the key from my back pocket, "give me back my phone."

"Yeah, I'll be back."

Chapter Twelve

Walking inside the hotel to leave the key the attendant, this is going to be a long ride home. Damn, she's so sexy when she gets mad. When we were married, some of our best sex was when she was mad at me. Trying to shake the thought from my head, the last thing I need is for her to see me with a hard on. Those damn jeans she's wearing are deadly. When she turned around to talk on the phone it took everything in me not to grab her ass. Feeling her phone vibrating, it's that prick Malcolm calling. Yeah, I've got to get rid of his ass real soon.

Still standing by the passenger door, she holds out her hand, "can I have my phone back now?"

Giving her back her phone as she's getting into the car, "your man just called. Are you hungry?"

"No." She says, closing the door while ignoring my comment about her man.

Getting into the car. "Just asking, we have a three hour drive ahead of us." Pulling out of the hotel, headed for the interstate, I glance over to see her texting someone. Probably his ass. Maybe I shouldn't have listened to Aiden. I've never done anything like this before and she's probably freaking out trying to figure out my next move.

"I'm trying to understand why you felt it necessary to go through all this trouble to talk. Whatever you have to say now, you could have said last night."

"You weren't trying to talk to me last night."

"I'm not trying to talk to you now, but I am."

"Not the same thing. Tell me about your man."

Turning to glare at me, "I don't think so." She says, with a frown on her face. "What else do you want to talk about?"

"You really want to know?" Staring at me, she doesn't respond. Blowing out a deep breath, "I'd like to talk about us. Look Michelle, I'm going to get straight to the point. I miss you." Rolling her eyes, she turns to look out the window. "Come on, don't you ever miss me? Miss what we had? Not all of our relationship was bad. We had some good times together."

Still looking out the window. "Sometimes, I think of the good times, but then I think of the bad." Turning to look at me, "Ronnie, I'm not really sure why you're saying all of *this*, but we're divorced. The only reason you probably miss me is because of the length of time that we were together. I don't know."

Nodding my head, "I'm sure that's some of it." Rubbing my hand down the back of my neck, "I guess I never thought in the beginning that our divorce would make me feel so empty." Oh shit! Did I mean to say that out loud? Judging by the look on her face, I shouldn't have said it quite so soon.

"I'm sure you haven't been sitting around for eleven months pining away over our failed marriage."

"I never said that I was pining away. Back to my question, tell me about your man?"

"Why?"

"I'm just asking. Is he someone I know?"

"I doubt it."

"So, you admit that you do have a man. Are you sleeping with him?"

Turning in her seat, she's scowling at me. "What? Why would you be asking me that?" Rolling her eyes, "are you still sleeping with Felecia?"

Briefly taking my eyes off the road, "you know good and damn well that I'm not seeing her ass anymore. Answer my question, are you sleeping with him or not?"

"Again, I'm not answering that. What *else* do you want to talk about?"

"Either you're sleeping with him or you're not. Why can't you answer?"

"I'm not answering because it's none of your business."

None of my business. Yeah, right. "Maybe I shouldn't say this, but I don't like the idea of you fucking around with some other guy."

"You're right, you shouldn't have said it. I haven't asked you who you've been fucking because I don't care. Is that what this whole returning my rental car so that we can talk crap is about?"

"Yes and no. I want to know what's going on with you."

Glaring at me, she shakes her head. "You want to know what's going on with me. Let's see." Looking out the window, she's biting on the inside of her bottom lip, left side, something she does when she's thinking or trying to process her thoughts, as she calls it. "I've been working a lot lately. I'm leaving for Hong Kong on Sunday and I'm not discussing anything other than that with *you*."

"Are you still mad at me?"

"No Ronnie. I'm not mad at you anymore."

"Part of what happened between us was just as much my fault as it was yours, Michelle. I shouldn't have been pressuring you for sex when I knew you weren't ready. And you're right, I was coming over that night to break up with you. I just wish you would've been honest with me."

"I was wrong for letting you think I was on the pill." She says, looking down at her hands. "I didn't want to lose you." Laughing through her nose, "in the midst of all of that was going wrong in my life, being with you felt right. You had everything that I thought I didn't have and needed. What I did was selfish and inconsiderate."

"In my heart, I always knew you were the one for me. But, I felt trapped. I wasn't ready for marriage *or* to be a parent and when you said that you were pregnant with my baby, I did what I had to do. I did what was right."

"It was still wrong of me to have put you in that type of predicament. I'm really sorry, Ronnie."

Entwining my hand with hers, "everything happens for a reason, right?"

Half smiling, "that's what my grandmother used to say."

"Feeling trapped was no excuse to cheat or behave the way that I did. I was a lousy husband and I'm sorry. You have no idea how sorry I am." Not responding to my last comment, she turns her head to look out the window again. At least she's not pulling her hand away. Squeezing her hand, "I forgive you."

Smiling, she turns to look at me. "I forgive you too."

Letting go of her hand, "*now,* can we be friends?"

Looking at me out the corner of her eye, "friends may be pushing it a little."

"At least I didn't say what I wanted to say."

"Which is what?"

"That I want my wife back."

Holding up her hand, "no, we can be friends."

"I can't have both?"

"No Ronnie, you can't have both."

"Alright, I'll settle for being your friend for now. Just know, Malcolm is about to be history."

"Is that what you think is going to happen?"

"That's what I know is going to happen. I don't share. Never have. Never will. You'll see."

"Whatever you say."

Chapter Thirteen

It's after five and I'm finally home. The ride wasn't so bad with the exception of Ronnie throwing out his subtle sexual hints here and there, throughout our conversation. It was actually good talking to him once the tension was gone. I don't know about us becoming friends again because I honestly don't see that happening. But, at least we're not at odds with each other anymore.

"Wow Michelle, your place is nice." He says, pulling up in front of my apartment. "When you said apartment, I was expecting an actual apartment complex, not a town home."

"Aren't they one in the same?"

Shaking his head, "no, they're not. You've always had a way of trying to downplay things."

Frowning at him, "I didn't downplay anything."

"Yes you did. You even have your own garage."

"I pay extra for that garage."

Getting my suitcase out of his trunk, "whatever. Are we going in through the garage to your *apartment* or the front door?" He's asking with sarcasm in his voice.

"You don't have to help me in. I'm sure you have other things to do." I say, trying to take my suitcase from him.

Pushing my hand away, "don't be ridiculous. When have I ever let you carry your own luggage?"

Ronnie is up to something. Walking ahead of him to the front door, "okay, well, I don't mean to be rude, but I have a lot to do, so you can't stay."

"Where would you like for me to put your suitcase?"

Still standing at the opened door, "you can leave it there."

Gesturing towards the door, "is there any reason why you haven't closed the door?"

"Yes, I already told you that you can't stay. I have to pack and prepare for my trip."

"You can't do that with me here? Or, is it that your man is coming over?"

Leaning against the door, "look, you need to leave." What the hell? Closing my front door, "Ronnie, what are you doing?"

"Getting comfortable. Where's the remote?"

"Are you serious? I tell you to leave and you just come in and sit down."

Patting the space beside him, "yep. Come sit with me. I won't be here long."

Closing my eyes, I have to take a deep breath to keep from going off. I don't know what's going on with him, but he's never behaved like this before. He's definitely up to something though. Holding up my left hand, "look Ronnie, I don't know what you're up to, but I don't have time for this today. I have a lot to do to prepare for my trip which means, you really need to leave." Seeing that he's not even making an attempt to move. "Fine," handing him the remote, "lock the door on your way out."

Taking my purse and bags into my bedroom, I begin to unpack. Ronnie is tripping. Big time. I'm going to ignore his ass. He has some nerve. And if this is his definition of our new friendship, he just gave me insight that I don't want it.

Chapter Fourteen

Laughing to myself, I know Michelle is pissed as hell. I've got to give it to Aiden, I like his way of thinking. Her cell phone just rang. It's probably Malcolm. Getting up from the sofa, her place is really nice. Spotless, just like our house when we were married. Entering her bedroom, she's standing in her closet talking on the phone. *"No. I'm okay. Yeah, I should have called you. No really, I'm okay. Don't come by. I'll see you tomorrow."* Laughing, *"I'm sure."* Going to stand behind her, I lean in to kiss her on the neck. Frowning, she quickly turns around as she's trying to push me away with her free hand, "Malcolm, can I call you back? Yeah, I won't take long." Pressing the end button on her phone, "what are you doing?"

"I came to check on you." Noticing that she's changed into a pair of cotton cut off shorts and a tank top, she looks good. I need to touch her, I can't resist. "I love your hair like this. It's so sexy. I loved your long hair, but short hair definitely looks good on you."

"Stop looking at me like that."

"How am I looking at you?"

Trying to walk past me, she shrugs her shoulders. "I don't know. You need to leave. I don't like…"

Pulling her by the waist, I grab the back of her head and start kissing her to cut off whatever it is she's about to say. Deepening the kiss, I suck her tongue into my mouth and start moving us towards her bed. Using my free hand to massage her breast, I've missed this so much. Moving from her lips to her neck, one of her sensitive spots, I go from nibbling to sucking. Hearing her moaning is like music to my ears.

"Wait Ronnie, we need to stop. We shouldn't... Ah, okay really. We need to, um, stop..."

Pulling her down onto the bed, I begin moving down her body. Lifting her tank top, I'm going from breast to breast, another sensitive area for her. Sucking her nipples deep into my mouth, Michelle has the perfect breast. They're perky and fit right into the palm of my hands. Pushing at my shoulders, she's moaning too much for me to stop. I know she's missed this just as much as I have. Still travelling south, I'm pulling down her shorts and underwear along the way. Knees planted on the floor, I pull her to the foot of the bed while placing her legs over my shoulders. So far, Aiden's been right so I might as well test out his white dude theory.

Chapter Fifteen

I know I'm going to regret doing this with Ronnie later. It feels too good and it's been so long, I'd be out of my mind to ask him to stop. He's performed oral sex on me many, many times before, but never like this. He's got my legs thrown over his shoulders and is holding me in place so that I can't move. Seeing his head bobbing up and down is freaky as hell! Feeling my orgasm coming on, I'm trying like hell to push him away because it's too much while holding him in place, because it feels so damn good! Throwing my head back, I have the one of the best orgasms I've ever had. Thinking he's going to stop, he's still going. I think I'm going to pass out. Breathing all hard, "Ronnie, ah Ronnie, oh my goodness, Ronnie please stop." Feeling him thrust his tongue in and out of my vagina is driving me insane!

Shit, Aiden was right. I have been licking and splitting. I'm enjoying the hell out of this. Michelle's squirming around and moaning has my dick damn hard. Inserting two fingers into her tight pussy, I feel her clenching my fingers signaling her second orgasm. Sucking her clit into my mouth, she's pushing at my shoulders and holding my head in place, not knowing that I wouldn't move even if she paid me a million dollars. It's just that good. Licking her clean, I'm already out of my jeans and underwear. Pulling my shirt over my head, I use my knee to push us up on the bed.

Pushing at Ronnie's chest before he can enter me, "Ronnie, wait. You need to put on a condom."

"Hell no. I'm not wearing a condom with my wife."

"I'm not your wife and if we're going to do this, you need a condom."

I'm horny as hell and she's trying to pull this shit. Getting up from the bed to retrieve a condom from my wallet, "this is bullshit Michelle. We've never used a condom before."

"We were married and I was on the pill then. On top of that, I don't know who you've been with. I'm not trying to catch a STD."

Settling myself between her legs, I'm going to keep my mouth shut. Staring her directly in the eyes while I'm entering her, for some strange reason, I've gotten emotional. It's like I've returned home. Not moving for a few minutes, she closes her eyes. The expression on her face is serene. Beginning to move, we're meeting each other thrust for thrust. Cupping her chin, I claim her lips. Using my tongue to mimic our movements is so damn erotic. Only with Michelle do I feel like this. Not able to hold back any longer, we reach our climax together. Rolling over to my side, she's staring up at the ceiling. "Hey, you okay?

"Yeah, I'm okay."

"Leaning up on my elbow, "you're not having any regrets are you?"

"Ronnie, I'm seeing someone." She says, sitting up in bed. "Of course, you know that already."

Staring at her, "maybe he's not that important to you after all. Be honest with me. You wanted this just as much as I did, didn't you?"

"It doesn't matter. It shouldn't have happened. I don't have random sex. Maybe you can do that, but I can't. It's wrong."

"Don't start. I haven't been with anyone in over seven months."

Looking down at me, "no matter how you look at it, if you have uncommitted sex, it's random."

"Michelle, we didn't have random sex. Apparently, you weren't listening to me earlier."

"I've heard everything you've had to say." Moving to get up from the bed, "I'm going to take a shower. If you want to clean up before you leave, you can use the bathroom upstairs."

"I can't take a shower with you?"

"No Ronnie, you can't. We can't do this again." *No matter how good it felt, I'm thinking to myself.*

"What? You're kidding, right?"

"I'm very serious."

Grabbing her by the wrist, "I don't want just sex from you Michelle. I want us. I've missed you. Being with you today feels right." Pulling her back down on the bed with me, "let me hold you for a few minutes."

Chapter Sixteen

Slowly opening my eyes to glance at the clock, it's six in the morning and my body aches. Ronnie had me in positions I don't recall ever being in when we were married. Moving his arm from around my waist, I climb out of bed to take a shower. Thinking I should wake him, I quickly change my mind. If I want to get anything done before my flight, I need to let him sleep. How did I allow this to happen? Going into my bathroom, I lock the door. Turning on the shower while waiting for my desired water temperature, I catch a glimpse of my reflection in the mirror. Oh my God, my chest is covered in hickeys. I should go out there and kick his ass! Glancing down at my stomach, oh hell, I have hickeys on my thighs too. Closing my eyes, I cannot let this happen again. I'm so glad that Malcolm didn't come over last night. I briefly spoke to him sometime during the night and told him that I was tired. Which wasn't a total lie.

Taking my shower, I must admit, I have missed the intimacy between us and he's right, our problems weren't in the bedroom, with the exception of him cheating. But still, I'm on a mission and that mission doesn't include Ronnie. Come to think of it, it doesn't include Malcolm either. I need to talk to Yolanda about this.

Coming out of the bathroom, wearing my spaghetti string towel wrap, Ronnie is still asleep. Going to the foot of the bed to look for my phone, there's a condom wrapper lying on the floor next to it. Looking around, I only see one condom wrapper. Shaking my head, surely he used condoms when he woke me up the other two times we had sex. Should I wake him up to ask? No, he did. He knows I'm no longer on the pill. Trying to remember if I could tell the difference from the first time we did it as compared to the other two times, I can't. Okay, calm down Michelle. Ronnie of all people wouldn't do anything like that. He doesn't want any kids. Deciding that I need to talk to Yolanda and gather the reports needed for my meeting in Hong Kong, I head upstairs to my office.
Two hours later...

Waking up from the most peaceful sleep I've had in months, I'm not ready to face reality. I heard Michelle while she was in the shower, but I was too tired to get up.

Getting out of bed, I grab my jeans as I'm heading into her bathroom to clean up.

Following the sound of the noise coming from upstairs, she must be in her office. Sounds like she's also on the phone.

"Hey, I called you earlier this morning. Where were you?" Laughing. "So you're still kicking it with Daren. Um hmm, I remember you telling me about that." I think she's on the phone with that skank, Yolanda.

"You won't believe what I did last night. Not with Malcolm. Ronnie. I know. Stop screaming. I know. I feel really bad. No, it was good but that doesn't matter, it was wrong. Shut up." She's not saying anything which means Yolanda must be giving her the "ho" lecture.

"He called me like three times. Yeah, I talked to him. Believe me, it was a very brief conversation. I'm just glad he didn't come over." Exhaling her breath, "the thing is, every time he tries... I just can't do it. I want to. You've seen him, he's fine as hell!" Laughing at something that skank is saying. "That's not it. Whatever! I know for a fact he's not as big as Ronnie. Because, I know. I felt it once or twice while we were dancing." Giggling into the phone. "I'd say he's about eight inches. Because I know. I'm a numbers woman, remember? Whatever. Seriously Yolanda, what should I do? What do I want to do? I have no idea, that's why I called you." Laying back on the floor, she wearing one of those towel dresses that she likes to wear after taking showers. "You're no help. I think what I'm going to do is avoid Ronnie. I'm not going backwards. We talked. Yeah, it was actually a good conversation. You already know, I have to be careful with him. Will you stop asking me that? Yes Yolanda, it was good. I think so. Well, he kept asking me if I've slept with Malcolm. No! Because, it's none of his business. Maybe he will. When he wakes up. Yeah, he's still here. Tell me what I should do and I'm not doing that. No! I'm going to hang up. Whatever. Bye!"

"What's none of my business?" I'm asking, walking into her office wearing nothing but my jeans.

Jumping at the sound of my voice, "why are you sneaking up on me like that?"

"I didn't sneak up on you. What's none of my business?"

Getting up from the floor, she walks over to her desk and starts putting some papers inside her briefcase. "When do you plan on getting dressed? You need to leave."

Walking over to the desk, "after we talk."

"Talk about what? We've already talked."

"Will you look at me?" Scowling, she looks up at me. "We need to talk about our relationship."

"Ronnie, we agreed to be friends. There's nothing more to discuss."

"We agreed to be friends before we made love. And if what I heard from your end of that conversation with Yolanda, your man hasn't gotten any and even if he has, he's history."

Exhaling a laugh, "are you on dope? Just because we had sex doesn't change anything between us." Closing her briefcase. "By the way, "what's up with all these damn hickeys?"

"It's called marking my territory, so you're little boyfriend knows his time is up."

"You are on dope if you... whatever. Anyways, I only saw one condom wrapper on the floor. What happened to the others?"

"I told you, I don't wear condoms with my wife."

"I. Am. Not. Your. Wife. Stop saying that and stop playing. Where are the other wrappers?"

Turning to leave her office, "There were no others. What time do you have to be at the airport?"

Chapter Seventeen

Following him out of my office, "Ronnie, please tell me you're playing. Please tell me you wore condoms." Not responding to me, I know he didn't do this. "Ronnie, oh my God! Why not? I told you I'm not on the pill anymore. What were you thinking? Why would you do something like that? Oh my God! I am so damn stupid! I knew I shouldn't have trusted your selfish ass!"

"Calm down." He says, walking into my bedroom. "Maybe you're not pregnant. If you are, we'll take care of our baby."

Oh no he didn't. "Have you lost your mind? I don't want a baby! You know what, get your clothes and get the hell out. I can't believe this shit. What was I thinking? I told your ass that I wasn't on the pill anymore and still, you would do something like this!"

"Michelle, will you calm the hell down. Damn! You acting like it's the end of the world. I wasn't thinking about using protection because you're my wife. I shouldn't have to wear a condom with my wife."

Yelling at the top of my voice, "I am not your wife! Stop saying that. We are not married!" Hearing my cellphone ring, I pick up before looking at the caller id, "what!" Oh shit, it's Malcolm. "Hey, I'm sorry. I'm not having a good morning. No, I'll be fine."

Standing behind me with his arms wrapped around my waist, "tell him you have a ride to the airport."

Turning out of Ronnie's hold, I walk over to my bed to find his shirt. Throwing it at him, while mouthing for him to leave, "no Malcolm, really, I'm fine."

Speaking louder, "Michelle, tell him that you don't need him to take you to the airport."

"Malcolm, I'm going to have to call you back. I'm trying to gather reports for my trip." Hanging up before he can respond. "Ronnie, get your ass out now! What the hell is wrong with you?"

Pulling his shirt over his head, "nothing's wrong with me. And if you don't want your boy to get hurt, you'd better call him back and tell him you don't need that ride."

"I'm not doing shit." Picking up his shoe and throwing it at him, "you just need to leave. And, as far as us being friends, that's not going to happen."

"Here you go with throwing shit again. I know we've had this conversation before."

Glaring at him, my cellphone rings again. Walking towards me like he's going to take the phone, "you better leave. I'm not playing with your ass."

"I'm not playing with your ass either."

"Ronnie, leave."

"Go ahead and answer."

Now my home phone is ringing and it's closer to him. Jumping up on my bed to get the phone, we reach for it at the same time. With the receiver in his hand, I'm trying to snatch it away from him and keep my balance from falling off the bed. Pushing me away, he's about to answer. Pressing the hang up button before he can say anything, he returns the phone to the cradle. Grabbing me around the waist, he slams me down on the bed. Remembering that I'm not wearing any panties, I reach to pull down the hem of my wrap. Grabbing me by my ankles, this fool has lost him damn mind!

"I tell you what, if you're going to let some fuck pick you up and take you to the airport, I want you to remember this. Lowering his head between my thighs, he starts sucking and licking me like a starved man. Trying to squirm out of his tight grasp is making him more aggressive. This orgasm is so intense, I've lost my damn voice. Getting up and kissing me on the lips. "I don't share Michelle. And if Malcolm is a real man, he's not going to like the idea of you fucking your husband." Hitting me on the ass, he leaves.

Picking up the phone to call Malcolm back, I assure him that everything is okay and tell him that I'll see him when he picks me up. Totally exhausted both mentally and physically, I'm looking forward to the long flight so that I can sleep. For now, I need to hurry and finish my packing, I'll worry over what happened with Ronnie later. I just pray I'm not pregnant. That's the last thing I need to happen in my very organized life where there's no room for him or a baby. Thinking about what Yolanda said earlier, she may be right. I think I'll always have a weakness for Ronnie. Shaking my head, this is too much to think about right now.

Chapter Eighteen

It's Thursday and I'm still mad at Michelle. Who in the hell is this Malcolm dude? Weak ass. Hearing my intercom buzzing, "yeah Rosie."

"Mr. Wen, I have your brother in law on the phone asking to speak with you."

Leaning back in my chair, "put him through." Pushing away from my desk, "what's up man?"

"Not much. I'm not going to hold you long, I'm checking to see how things went with Michelle?"

Laughing out loud, "man, I don't know. They were going good until she started acting crazy and having regrets."

"Regrets about what?"

"Cheating on that prick. By the way, I saw his ass when he came to take her to the airport."

"Were you there when he picked her up?"

"Yeah, but she doesn't know I was there."

"Did you jack his ass up?"

"Nah man, I parked near her house so I could see what he looked like." Hearing him grunt into the phone, "She was already tripping so I didn't want to make matters worse."

"Fuck that, he wouldn't have taken my woman to the airport. I would have met his ass at the door and let him know that his time for playing house with my woman was over."

"Don't think the thought didn't cross my mind. I did find out that she hasn't slept with him though and knowing Michelle, she won't."

"How do you know she hasn't slept with him?"

"I overheard her on the phone talking to her friend."

"You go white guy on her?"

Smiling to myself, "I'm not telling you anything beyond what I've already told you."

"Ha, ha, you did that's why you're pissed."

"Now, why would I be pissed about doing that?"

"You're pissed because after all that you did, and I know you did, she still let some fucker take her to the airport. The thing is, you can't give up. She's tough and it's going to take a little more to break down her defenses."

"I'm not giving up." I dare not tell him that she might be pregnant. Both times that I woke her up, a condom was the last thing on my mind. All I wanted was her with no barriers between us and she felt so damn good. I'm getting a hard on just thinking about her.

"When is she scheduled to return?"

"She said she'd be gone for seven days so she'll be back on Sunday."

"Are you picking her up from the airport?"

"I hadn't planned on it."

"Then I tell you what, that guy is probably going to pick her up. You need to do something to make your presence known. She's for sure not going to tell him that she slept with her ex so you've got to tell him."

Laughing, "I'm taking your advice when I should be kicking your ass because I know that you used these same tactics on my sister."

Sounding all proud, "I did, and don't forget that your sister and I are happily married with two beautiful children. Well anyways, I was just checking on you, I've got to get back to work."

"Alright man, I'll talk to you later."

Hanging up the phone, I'm done for the day. I think I'm going to take Aiden's advice and work on getting rid of that damn Malcolm so I can get my woman back.

Chapter Nineteen

Finally, I'm back in San Diego waiting to get clearance to exit the plane. The meeting in Hong Kong went a lot better than expected. Felton and I were able to secure the contract and all is well. At least, I hope all is well. It took me about two days to gather my thoughts concerning Ronnie and the possibility of being pregnant. I came to the conclusion that having sex with him again would be detrimental to my mind. I don't need the drama. And if I'm pregnant, which I pray that I'm not, I'll just have to deal with it.

Hearing the flight attendant say that we're cleared to exit the plane, I'm headed directly to baggage claims. After being on this plane for over seventeen hours, I still have a serious case of jet lag from the first trip. I sent Malcolm a text while I was on the plane confirming that he's still going to pick me up. Waiting for my bags, I think back to our conversation on last Sunday when he picked me up for the airport...

"Good morning beautiful," he said when he arrived.

"Good morning."

Closing the door behind him, *"what was going on earlier when I called? I thought I heard someone's voice in the background."*

"I was having a disagreement with my ex-husband. It was nothing."

Looking at me like he's trying to decipher if he should press the issue or not, *"was he here with you?"*

"Yeah, he stopped by." There's no need to tell him when he stopped by. *"Like I said, it was nothing."*

Slowly nodding his head, *"I could tell that you were irritated. But, I guess that's what exes do. Oh well, you ready to go?"*

Staring at him, I can't believe that's all he's going to say? Fine with me. I think I've met my fool quota for the day. Grabbing my business satchel and purse, I open the door for him to pass with my luggage before setting the alarm.

Our ride to the airport was relatively quiet, which was also okay. It was when we arrived that he threw in the whammy on me, *"you know Michelle, we've been going out for a few months now and although I haven't pressed the issue of intimacy too much, I want you to know that I'm really digging you. I'm not trying to rush things and I know that you're busy with work, but I'd like to know how you view our relationship?"*

What? Why would he spring something like this on me now? Exhaling a deep breath, I can see the sincerity in his eyes. However, after being with Ronnie and having to deal with his craziness, the last thing on my mind is sex. *"Malcolm, I really like you a lot. But, as I told you in the beginning, I don't want to get seriously involved with anyone right now. Not to mention, sex is a big step."*

Nodding his head, *"you told me that three months ago and at the time I accepted your answer because I thought you were still getting over your divorce. But the more time I spend with you, I see that's not the case. I want more. Am I not someone you see yourself dating seriously?"*

Hell yes! You're fine as hell! *"That's not it. It's just that I don't want to move too fast and then regret my decision later. I think you're a great guy and I don't want to ruin our friendship by moving towards something that I know I'm not ready for."*

"Are you sure your answer has absolutely nothing to do with your ex?"

"No! Why would you ask me that?"

"You just look and seem different this morning. I don't know. I'm not liking this vibe between us."

The vibe between us? "I'm not sure what you're feeling Malcolm. If I'm different, it's because I'm stressed about this meeting." What is up with these guys this morning? Damn! "Look, I need to get going."

Staring at me with a blank expression on his face, "yeah, I'll get your bags from the trunk." Passing my luggage to the skycap, he turns to face me, "have a safe trip and I'll see you when you get back." Looking down at me, he gives me a quick kiss on the lips. Hugging me, he walks away.

It wasn't until I arrived in Hong Kong that I noticed the hickey in the crook of my neck while washing my face before going to bed on Tuesday night. That was what Malcolm was probably staring at. However, he never said anything about it in the two conversations we had over the phone or in the numerous text messages so like him, I'm not going to say anything about it.

Pulling my bag off the belt, I see Malcolm waiting by the curb at passenger pick up. "Hey babe, how was your trip home?"

Smiling at him, "long and tiring. I'm so glad to be back home."

Kissing me on the lips as he's taking my luggage, he's wearing jeans and a pullover sweater. Malcolm is really a handsome man. His dark complexion is like looking at smooth milk chocolate. He's a little shorter than Ronnie and slightly thicker, but still fine. "I would ask if you'd like to hang out with me today, but I know you're tired, so I'll give you a pass." He says, with a wink.

"Thanks for the pass. I can almost promise you I won't be good company."

On the way to my apartment, he's filling me in on what's been going on with his business and I tell him about my meeting in Hong Kong as well as some of the places that Felton and I visited after our meetings. Hong Kong is really a beautiful city and the facility that is being built is going to be awesome.

Approaching my apartment, there's a florist van parked in my driveway. I have a sinking feeling like something is about to go wrong. Parking beside the van, the driver gets out first. Waiting for me to get out of Malcolm's car, he says, "hi ma'am, I have a delivery for you that requires a signature." Signing for the flowers, "thank you ma'am, this may take a while so I'll go ahead and unload the van, if it's okay with you. Nodding my head, I can see Malcolm's pissed expression. Apparently, the flowers aren't from him.

Unlocking the door to enter my house, both Malcolm and the delivery guy are right on my heels. After about the forth vase filled with roses, each with a card that I dare not read in front of Malcolm, he says, "Michelle, what the hell is going on? Who are these roses from?"

Shrugging my shoulders, "I don't know."

Frowning at me, "you can easily find out by reading the card."

Walking over to retrieve one of the cards, the roses are from Ronnie. Oh God...

> *Michelle, I'm serious about what I said.*
> *I don't share and I'm not giving up.   Ronnie*

"What does it say?"

"Nothing important." Damn, I just need to tell him. "Listen Malcolm, they're from my ex."

Pacing back and forth in front of me, "your ex, huh? So your ex sends you what..." Looking around as he's counting, "seven dozens of roses and you act like it's not a big deal. On a Sunday? Who the hell delivers roses on Sundays?"

"It's not a big deal to me. We're divorced."

Letting out a frustrated chuckle, "don't lie to me Michelle. Just tell me, are you still seeing your ex?"

He's pissing me off and I know that Ronnie did this on purpose. "Look, I've already told you that there's nothing going on between us. I don't know why he did this and I don't care." Taking a deep breath, "either you believe me or you don't. I can't control what he does."

Pulling me into a hug, "I believe you. But, I need you to see it through my eyes. How would you feel if you came to my place and were exposed to the same thing?"

"I wouldn't like it, but I'd believe you, if I knew you were telling me the truth."

Pulling back just a little, "I'm not going to trip. I know you're tired, so I'm going to let you get some rest. Hey, why don't we get together Friday and check out Macey's House of Rhythm & Blues?"

Smiling at his gesture, "that sounds like fun." Looking up into his eyes, "Malcolm, I know that deep down you don't believe me and honestly, I probably wouldn't believe me either. But I'm telling you, there is nothing going on between me and Ronnie."

Taking his thumb to rub the rim of my lower lip, "I believe you, Michelle. I guess I'm a little uncomfortable with your ex-husband all of a sudden showing interest in you again." Blowing out a deep breath, "look. I hear you and I'm not going to sweat it. Okay?"

Pulling his hand away, I push up on my toes to give him a kiss. "Okay."

"Well, I'm going to get going *unless* you want me to stay." He says, with his eyebrows raised.

Shrugging my shoulder, "if you want to stay, you're more than welcome." Had Ronnie not sent those damn roses to try and show me up, he would've been gone a long time ago.

"No, I better go. For what I have in mind, I'd better go."

Giving him a tight lipped smile, it doesn't matter what he has in mind, because I'm not giving him anything. I already told him that. "Yeah, you should probably go. I'm going to unpack and try to get some rest." Total lie. As soon as he leaves, I'm going to call Ronnie and cuss his ass out for sending all these damn roses.

"Alright. Remember, if you get lonely later, call me. You know I'll come right over."

Ushering him out the door, he's getting on my last damn nerve. Will you leave already? "Yeah, I'll keep that in mind. Talk to you later." Closing the door behind him, I'm in search of my phone.

Answering the phone on the second ring, "hey babe my ass!"

Chapter Twenty

Tonight, against my better judgment, I'm going out on a double date with my frat brother, Chad. After sharing with him how Michelle overreacted about the roses that I had sent to her, he suggested that I needed to get out. I'm still pissed at her ass. I spent over $500 on those damn roses. I don't give a fuck about Malcolm being there when they were delivered. I wanted him to see that time is running out for his ass.

"Man, I'm telling you, Kari's friend, Trina, is fine as frog's hair. I know for a fact she's a freak."

"I hear you. So what time do I need to be at Macey's?"

"Stop sounding so drab. You just need to give Michelle some time. She'll come around. Shit, Trina is just something to do in the meantime."

"Drab? What kind of word is that? By the way, is this the same Trina who Tony was fucking around with a few weeks ago?"

"Yeah, that's her. Why?"

"Tony told me about her ass. If I go, you're footing the bill."

"Man, what? Why do I need to foot your bill?"

"I'm not spending my money on that skank so you can impress Kari."

"That's just wrong. I already told you that the only reason she agreed to go out with me was if I could find someone to go out with ole girl."

"Like I said, I'll go, but I'm not spending my money on her ass."

"Fine, be there at seven."

Arriving at Macey's, Chad and the ladies are already here waiting for me. He didn't lie, they are fine as hell.

"Hey Ronnie, this is Trina and of course, you've already met Kari. Just as I'm about to say something to Trina, the waiter comes to take us to our seats. Macey's is like an upscale lounge with semi-round table booths with a small stage front and center. It's a very cozy environment for real couples.

Glancing down at the drink menu, Chad and the ladies are talking about all the drink choices and their ingredients. Clearing his throat, I look up at Chad as he's motioning for me to look towards the door. What the hell? Michelle is here with Malcolm. And why is she wearing that short ass dress?

Touching my arm, "so Ronnie, what are you going to order?" Trina is asking, sounding like she has a fucking frog in her throat.

Staring at Michelle, who is now sitting two tables over from us, "I don't know."

"Are you alright?"

Moving my arm, "yeah, I'm fine." I know Michelle sees me staring at her. Getting up from the table, "excuse me, I'll be back." Walking past their table, I slow my pace until our eyes meet. Nodding at her, she quickly looks away.

"Excuse me, Malcolm. I need to go to the ladies room." I can't believe Ronnie's here. I saw him when we first walked in. I was hoping that we would be seated on the other side of the room, but Malcolm insisted that we be seated in front of the stage. Damn!

Walking towards the restroom, Ronnie is leaning against the wall. "Hey."

"Hey. I like what you're wearing."

"Thanks."

"A little short to be wearing for someone who's never going to get the chance to get any, don't you think?"

"Ronnie, there is nothing wrong with this dress. And how do you know he's not going to get any?"

Walking towards me, "because it's mine." He says, pushing me into the corner so that his back is to anyone going into the restrooms.

"You're tripping. Aren't you here with someone?"

"I don't give a damn about that skank. I'm only here because Chad is trying to impress his girl."

Staring up at him, "well I'm going back…"

I can't let her go back out there without getting a kiss from her. Grabbing her by the waist, I capture her mouth in a kiss. Palming her butt, "I want to see you tonight."

Looking up at me with our lips mere inches apart, "Ronnie, I need to go back out there."

"Tonight, Michelle. I want to see you tonight."

Licking her bottom lip before pulling it into my mouth, I lightly suck before sweeping my tongue inside her mouth. "Tonight." Grinding my center into her, "I want you. Tonight."

Bringing her arms to wrap around my neck, "Ronnie, you know I can't do that. I'm here with Malcolm."

Placing my hands on her hips, "I don't care how you make it happen, I want to see you tonight. Either you say yes or we can go out there together and tell him what happened on Saturday."

Pulling back from me, "really, you're threatening me?"

"I told you, I don't share."

"I'm not yours to share."

"You'll always belong to me. So are you going to meet me tonight, at the house, or do we need to go out there and have a talk with your boy?"

Scowling at me, "okay." She says, through clenched teeth. "I can't believe you're doing this. And what's worse, I think you'd really go out there and tell him what happened."

"Damn right I will and be careful how you sit in that short ass dress. I don't want him getting the wrong idea."

Rolling my eyes at him, I storm into the restroom. I can't believe his ass. Looking in the mirror, my lips look like I've been kissed. Damn, I forgot my purse. Shrugging my shoulders, oh well.

Going back to our table, I keep my eyes trained on Malcolm although, I can feel Ronnie glaring at me. Asshole!

The lights are now dimmed in the restaurant, signaling the performer's entrance. Watching Michelle as she's approaching their table, she looks good as hell wearing that short, off the shoulder black dress with black stiletto heels. When she walked into that standing area, I was tempted to push her into the restroom and screw the hell out of her, which is exactly what I'm going to do later tonight.

Luckily, she's sitting where I can see her face. I'm so focused on Michelle that I've completely tuned out this cackling chick sitting next to me.

"Ronnie, I'm talking to you."

Slowly turning to face her, "what?"

Frowning at Kari, "I was asking you if you wanted to dance."

"No. I don't want to dance."

Chad, looking like he's about to stroke out, "man, are you okay?" He's asking with a nervous laugh."

"I'm fine." I'm saying as the waitress approaches our table to take our orders. Ordering a steak, compliments of Chad, I notice that there's also a waitress at Michelle's table taking their order. I wonder what she's ordering.

Sitting back in my seat, the singer gets up on the stage and starts singing, 'Sweet Thing.' Glancing up at Michelle, we both smile. When we were in college, this was our song. Staring at each other, we're in our moment. Then out of the blue the singer belts out, 'Tonight is the Night.' Oh hell, this is memory lane. When I was trying to talk her into having sex, we listened to this song over and over. It was my way of showing her what to expect. Staring at me with that mischievous smile of hers, she's right there with me. Maybe it was a good thing that I came here tonight. I'll have to thank Chad later for his role in our foreplay.

It's like someone is playing a trick on me tonight. I swear. Here I am sitting with Malcolm, while my whole being is attached to Ronnie. If it wasn't bad enough sitting here listening to 'Tonight is the Night' and 'Sweet Thing,' I'm about to stroke out listening to R. Kelly's, 12 play. I'm trying my best to keep my eyes focused on Malcolm but as the song goes on, I can see and hear Ronnie doing everything the song says. Watching Ronnie, take his bottom lip into his mouth and slowly pulling it out is causing crazy things to happen down below.

Frowning at me, "Michelle, are you okay?"

Tearing my gaze away from Ronnie, I clear my throat, "umm hmm, why do you ask?"

"You're breathing really hard."

No, I'm not okay. I'm ready for this boring ass date to be over so that Ronnie can give me some of his 12 play is what I want to scream! "I'm fine, just feeling a little congested."

"Oh, I thought this song may have had something to do with it."

Staring down at my meal, "no, I'm just a little congested."

"You know Michelle, I can give you what this song is offering."

Looking up and meeting his eyes, I'll bet you can. The thing is, you're not Ronnie. What the hell is wrong with me? Ronnie messed up. "I thought we agreed to wait."

Clearly pissed, "well, you can't blame a guy for trying."

Still staring at him, "I guess I can't."

"How long are we going to wait? I mean, I've never asked before, but do you have some 90 day rule?"

"Malcolm, I don't want to ruin our relationship by having sex."

"You honestly think that will happen with us?"

Shrugging my shoulders, "I don't know. People do change after having sex."

"You know that's the idea right? People have sex to get closer." Leaning back and placing his arm behind my head, he rubs my hair, "I'm really attracted to you. If I change, it will be for the better. You should know by now that I'm not like most men."

Looking past Malcolm, I see Ronnie leaning forward in his seat. Diverting my attention back to Malcolm. "That's easy for you to say now." Glancing back over at Ronnie. I can't believe I'm about to say this. "Look Malcolm, I'm not ready to have sex with you. I don't even know when or I'll ever be ready. So, if you're looking for intimacy…"

Abruptly standing up, "you know what," he says, "forget I said anything. Are you ready to go?"

Sliding out of the booth, "yeah, I'm ready."

Walking past Ronnie's table, Malcolm has his hand on the small of my back. Whispering in my ear, "too bad you're holding out. This dress is killing me." Judging by the look on Ronnie's face, I think he heard him.

Chapter Twenty One

Moving to get up to leave, "hey man, I'm out. Trina, it was nice meeting you."

"Wait, you're leaving?" Looking over at Kari, "I thought we were hooking up tonight."

"Who told you that we were hooking up?"

"I, I was just under the impression that we were."

Staring at Chad, "I don't know what you were told, but I'm not trying to *hook up* with anybody."

"Kari, babe, I thought we talked about this." Chad says, looking all nervous and shit.

"No, Chad. We didn't."

"You know what? This is some bullshit. You've sit here all night and ignored me. Thought I didn't peep your ass staring at that chick who was sitting at the other table. Man, I was doing you a favor. You see this body? I can have anybody I want."

This bitch! "You did me a favor? Bitch, I did you a favor. You're right, you've been *had* alright. Remember Tony? Yeah, he told me about your nasty stank ass."

"Did he just call her a bitch?" Kari is asking Chad.

"Yeah, I called your skank ass friend a bitch." Getting up from the table, "Chad man, I'm sorry. I'm not about to sit here and deal with this shit. I'm out."

Chapter Twenty Two

Arriving at Ronnie's, I'm feeling really bad about the way I treated Malcolm tonight. Especially, when he dropped me off at home. Instead of letting him come inside, I leaned over and kissed him on the cheek and told him good night. All because I saw Ronnie leaving the club and didn't want to risk him coming to my apartment.

Hitting myself on the forehead with the palm of my hand, what in the hell am I thinking? Ronnie doesn't own me. He doesn't have the right to call the shots like this. So what if he tells Malcolm. I don't owe him anything either.

Staring at the garage, maybe I should go back home. If I let Ronnie start doing this to me, he'll think he has some kind of power over me.

Decision made, I'm going back home.

Where in the hell is Michelle? She left that club over two hours ago. Looking at my watch, she should have been here by now. Going into the kitchen to get my cell...

"Where are you?"

"At home."

"You're on your way, right?" Why is she still at home?

"Nope." She says, with much attitude. "You don't get to have that kind of control over me."

"Control you? I'm not trying to control you." Going silent for a few seconds, oh yell nah! "Michelle, don't tell me you slept with that fucker. I saw his hand all over your ass."

"What?" She says, laughing. "If you saw his hand all over my behind, then not only do you need to have your head examined, you might want to get your eyes checked too."

"Don't laugh at me. There's not a damn thing funny."

"Yeah, whatever." She responds, yawning. I'm going to bed."

"Hold up. What you need to do is get your ass over here like we planned."

"You mean like you planned? You tried to blackmail me. In the past, that probably would have worked with the old Michelle. Just so you know, she's long gone."

"Well you need to find her and bring her ass back."

Giggling into the phone, "good night, Ronnie."

I'm pissed and horny as hell. I can't believe she called my bluff. Let me try another approach. Whispering into the phone, "babe, you're right, I was wrong for trying to manipulate you into coming over. I saw you in that dress and had a brief moment of insanity."

Sighing, "Ronnie, I think we need to go back to the way we were."

"The way we were? You mean not talking at all?"

"There's a reason why we're divorced."

"Babe, I've already apologized for messing up. Don't do this. We can start over."

"Why should I make changes in my life for you? How do I know that you've even changed? You think that because we slept together that everything is ok. But, it's not. What we did was wrong and it should have never happened."

Rubbing my hand down my face, I don't like the direction of this conversation. "So, what are you telling me?"

"I'm telling you that I'm not changing my life for you. We're no longer married and I don't owe you anything. Malcolm is a good man. If I decide not to see him anymore, it's going to be my decision, not yours."

Speaking into the phone, my tone barely above a whisper, "Michelle, I have changed. My biggest regret is that I ruined our marriage. I want you back."

Sniffling into the phone, "Ronnie, I'm going to hang up now."

"Alright. Just know, I'm not giving up. I know what I want. You keep that in mind. I went about tonight the wrong way, but it doesn't change how I feel about you."

Chapter Twenty Three

It's been almost three weeks now since I last talked to Ronnie. As much as I hate to admit it, I miss him. But, as much as I miss him, I know in my heart that going backwards isn't wise.

When I last spoke to him, he said that he's changed. I'm not so sure if he's telling the truth. The way that he's behaved this past month or so, reminds me of the same old Ronnie who I was married to. The one who feels that the world revolves around him.

What I told him was true, Malcolm is a good man. He treats me well and he hasn't deserved how I've been treating him. Tonight, he's invited me over for dinner. He swears that he can cook so I'm going to see if his food measures up to all the bragging he's been doing. I told him that I would be at his house around seven.

Opening the door for me, he kisses me on the lips. "You're just in time."

"Smells good in here." Following him into the kitchen, "what are you cooking again?"

Turning to face me, "you don't like surprises, do you?"

Shrugging my shoulders, "no, not really."

Smirking at me, "well as cute as you are, you're going to have to wait until you're served."

"Cute, huh?"

"And sexy." He says, winking at me. "Would you like a glass of wine?"

"Sure." I love Malcolm's kitchen. He has this huge island that has a half stove and sink on one end and the remainder is sleek, black granite that looks like glass. Rubbing my hand over his island, he's staring at me. "Don't worry, I'll wipe off my fingerprints."

"That's not what I'm thinking." He says, in a low tone, while handing me my glass of wine.

Taking a sip, "what are you thinking?"

Shaking his head, "it's probably best that I keep that thought to myself."

Coming to stand next to me, he's wearing a black cotton shirt and jeans. This man is hella fine. But not as fine as Ronnie. Taking another sip of my wine. What is wrong with me? Turning to lean my back against the island, "so, you're really not going to tell what you're cooking for dinner?"

"Nope." Placing his wine glass on the island, he lightly rubs his hand down the back of my head. "I love your hair, Michelle. It's so soft."

Playfully frowning at him, "I've noticed. You're always touching it. I guess no one ever told you that us black women don't like having our hair touched."

Throwing his head back in a chuckle, "so I've heard." Looking at me out the corner of his eye, "I love your lips too. They're soft as well."

If this is his way of trying to seduce me, it's working. I like this relaxed, sexy, bad boy side of Malcolm. Nodding at him, I don't respond.

"I also like this dress you're wearing tonight." He says, skimming his finger across the neck line.

I chose to wear a black and white maxi dress tonight since we aren't going out, with sandals. Trying not to sound all breathless, "um thanks. Is the food almost ready?"

Looking at me with hooded eyes, he nods. Capturing my chin, he pushes my head back to meet his lips while taking the wine glass from my hand and placing it on the island. "You're so beautiful. I don't think you even realize the power you have."

Breathing heavy because he's too close, "what kind of power?"

"The power to make men fall at your feet. The power that even though I don't always agree with your logic, I'll do almost anything just to be with you."

"Wow, that's some power." I respond, in almost a whisper.

Nodding at me, "yeah, it is. That's what makes you so special." Leaning down, he takes my mouth into a kiss so sensuous that I feel it's affect in the pit of my stomach. "I want you so badly, Michelle. I've heard what you've been saying about sex changing people and like I've told you, I'm not like most men. I can get sex anywhere, at any time but that's not what I'm about." Kissing me again, I feel him lifting me onto the island. "If you want to wait, I'll wait." He says against my lips. "I'm not going to lie to you though, it's getting really hard to be around you and not be able to fully express myself."

What do I do? There's a part of me that wants him just as bad. Then, there's a part of me that knows that I'm not ready yet. I'm still relishing in the fact that I'm not pregnant from my little tryst with Ronnie. Taking a deep breath, I do something that I've never done with any man with the exception of Ronnie. Closing my eyes, I have so many emotions going on in my mind. Looking up to meet his eyes, I nod my answer.

Not wasting anytime, Malcolm spreads my legs as wide as my dress will allow. Pulling me into another kiss, his hands are everywhere. Briefly, I feel my feet hit the ground before being lifted back onto the island in nothing but my black bra and panties. Kissing down the side of my neck, he's squeezing my breast. "Your body is so beautiful." He says, while capturing my nipple and pulling it into his mouth with my bra still intact. Returning to my lips, I feel him unclasping my bra. I'm wondering how he feels about my breast. Ronnie never complained about my 32B size. "Your breasts are perfect." He says, as he sucks my nipple into my mouth. Travelling down my body, this feels so good! Lying me back on the island, he trails his hands, followed by his lips from my neck all the way down to my belly button while lifting my hips to remove my panties. At the first contact of his mouth on my center, I'm literally melting. Oh my goodness, this feels so good!

I'm trying my best to stay still. I'm trying my absolute best not to scream! Oh hell, it's not working. If I thought Ronnie could eat cat, I now know – he has some serious competition.

Hearing Malcolm moaning, I take it that he's enjoying this as much as I am. Lifting me off the island, he has my coochie smack dab in his face while he's still feasting. Lying me down on his bed, he still hasn't stopped. Finally, he raises up and my entire body is throbbing. "I knew you would be good." He says, while leaning over to retrieve a condom from his bedside table.

Maybe I should stop him. As bad as I want this, my emotions are all over the place. Before I can even get the word out, he's inside of me. Not moving, I glance up to see his expression. Finding his eyes closed and lips slightly parted, he says, "give me a minute. It's been a while and I really want to enjoy this and not have you thinking that I'm a ten second brotha."

Laughing at his comment, he begins to move. Oh my goodness, can he move. Meeting him, thrust for thrust, I feel my orgasm slowly coming. Throwing my head back as I cum, a steady stream of tears are flowing down the sides of my face.

Grunting his release, he looks down at me. "Hey, why the tears?"

Not able to say anything, I shake my head.

"Baby, I didn't hurt you, did I?"

Still not able to form the words to say what I feel, I just shake my head.

Pulling out of me, he moves to the side of the bed to remove the condom and steps back into his jeans. Looking back at me, "you know this a blow to my ego right?" Staring at me for a few minutes, he rubs his hand down the back of his head. "Michelle, I should have known you weren't ready for this. You tried to tell me so many times. I was being selfish and I'm sorry. The last thing I've ever wanted to do was rush you or pressure you and I guess I failed."

Sitting up in the bed, "it's not your fault." Taking a deep breath as fresh tears start to flow, "how do you even know what I'm crying about?"

"I've been there before." Walking out of the room, he returns with my clothes. "At least tell me it was good."

"It was better than good. Could you not tell by all the noise I made?"

Coming to sit on the bed beside me, "nah, I think I was screaming just as loud."

Laughing with him, I'm still really emotional. Touching his arm, "Malcolm, I wanted this as much as you did." Taking a deep breath in an attempt to hold my tears at bay, "I've never been with any other man with the exception of Ronnie. I don't have random sex. I've always felt that people should be committed to each other before they're intimate." I dare not tell him what I'm really feeling. I just shared a part of myself with a man who I care a great deal for but that's the extent of my feelings for him. This was just random sex.

Going into the bathroom to get dressed, I come out to find an empty room. Going into the kitchen, he has our dinner set up on the island where we just had sex. "Are we going to eat here, at the island?"

Smiling at me, "I was thinking that we could. Is it okay with you?"

Trying not to offend him, "aren't you going to clean it off first?"

Sitting down, while patting the bar stool next to him, "nah, you might decide not to give me anymore so all I have is this island as a reminder."

"That is so gross!"

"Believe me, it was delicious."

Chapter Twenty Four

It's been a minute since I last talked to Michelle and I really miss her. I have to admit, I was pissed at her for choosing Malcolm over me, but I'm still not giving up.

I was up in the attic looking for some old finance books on yesterday and came across some pictures of us when we first started dating. We were so carefree then and even though I cheated, I always treated Michelle like my princess.

With it being Saturday, I thought to call her first but ruled that out because I didn't want to hear over the phone that she doesn't want to see me. I need to see her eyes. I know she still has feelings for me and I need to do all that I can to make her realize that.

Knocking on the door, I laugh to myself recalling Michelle telling me that she lives in an apartment. I can only imagine how much she pays for this *apartment* with her own front and back yard. Yeah, it's an apartment all right.

Hearing her unlock the door, "hey, why are you here?"

Has she been crying? Holding up the photo album, "I found these in the attic and thought I'd bring them to you."

Looking down at her feet, she holds out her hand. "Okay, thanks for bringing them by."

Grabbing her hand, "Michelle, what's wrong?"

Not pulling her hand away, "nothing, just got a lot on my mind."

Staring at her, "I was actually thinking we could look at these together. Is it okay for me to come inside?"

Turning to walk into her *apartment*, I close the door behind me and follow her into her family room. She's wearing some thigh length blue jean shorts and a black tee shirt. Sitting on the sofa beside her, "what's going on?"

Finally, she meets my eyes and my heart breaks into a million pieces. "Nothing that I care to discuss. Let me see the pictures."

After about the fourth picture, one of me frowning at Yolanda, she starts to laugh. "Don't laugh. I still hate that girl."

"Yeah, well she's not too fond of you either."

"We were all over each other when were in school. Remember?" Noticing that in all of our pictures, we either hugging, kissing or standing so close to each other that not even air could get between us.

Nodding her head, she wipes away a tear. "Um hmm, we were." She says, with emotion in her voice.

Coming to a picture of what I think is us at a Valentine's Day dance, I'm standing behind her with my arms wrapped around her waist as she's looking up at me. Smiling at the picture, I glance over to see a steady stream of tears. "Baby, what's wrong?" I want to think it's the pictures, but she seemed upset when she opened the door. "Did something happen?" I'm almost afraid of her answer. Whatever it is, I have a feeling that I'm not going to like it.

"I don't want to talk about it." She says, staring at the television which I now notice has the volume turned down.

Damn, I don't want to ask. Shit! "Did something happen between you and Malcolm?" Oh my God, that look. That look says it all. Dropping my head in my hands, "please tell me you didn't do what I think you did."

Sobbing, she doesn't say anything. Wiping at her tears, she gets up and goes into her bedroom.

Sitting here on the sofa, I can't move. I feel like someone just kicked me in the stomach. Rubbing my eyes, I need to pull myself together for her. I'm not really sure how can I go in there and comfort her when there's a part of me that wants to choke the hell out of her for sleeping with another dude. Then, there's a part that wants to go find Malcolm and kill his ass. And finally, there's the part that says that this is all my fault. I did this to us. I know how Michelle feels about sex. She hasn't changed.

Walking into her bedroom, she's laying there in a fetal position. Lying in bed beside her, "baby, please don't cry. Did he hurt you?" Shaking her head no. I wonder if she enjoyed it. Shaking my head, I hope like hell she didn't. Rubbing her arm, "did he force you to have sex with him?"

"No Ronnie, he didn't." Taking a deep breath, "it was random sex. I had sex with a man who I don't love. I gave him a part of me that I can't get back and I'm just really disappointed in myself. I knew I wasn't ready and I got caught up in the moment."

Oh God. Please help me. It was one thing when I thought I knew what happened but for her to admit that she slept with him, it hurts like hell. Just holding her, "does Malcolm know how you feel?"

"I told him."

"What did he say?"

Turning onto her back, "he thinks I have hang ups."

"What kind of hang ups?"

Looking at me, she doesn't say anything.

"So, I'm your hang up?"

Staring up at her ceiling, "it doesn't matter."

Exhaling my breath, "listen Michelle, in time you'll feel better." I've got to get out of here. "Listen, I'm going home. Call me if you need anything." Not giving her time to respond, I'm out.

Arriving home, I'm raging on the inside. Why did she sleep with him? Punching the wall in my bedroom. Damn! I'm yelling. How could she allow some man to touch what belongs to me? I told her that I don't share. I've told her over and over that I don't share. Punching the wall again, she deserves to hurt. She needs to hurt like I'm hurting. You know what, fuck her! I don't need this shit.

Sitting on my bed, all I can do is cry. I can't believe she did this us. She knew how I felt. I told her how I felt. Laying back on the bed, damn! I'm yelling. Why did she do this?

Chapter Twenty Five

"Mr. Wen, I've been trying to reach you over the intercom for the last fifteen minutes."

Turning from facing the window, "sorry Rosie, what do you need."

Suspiciously eyeing me, "I wanted to let you know that your two o'clock appointment is running late."

Pressing some buttons on my computer, "thanks Rosie. Let me know when he gets here."

Coming into my office and closing the door, "Ronnie, what's going on? You've been moping around here like you've lost your best friend. I've never seen you like this before."

"Rosie, have you ever lost something of value?"

"As a matter of fact, I have."

"The thing is, when I had this jewel, I didn't properly take care of it and now it's gone."

Holding up her hand, "let me ask you this so that I fully understand, are we talking about an item or a person?"

Speaking barely above a whisper, "a person."

"Um hmm. This person wouldn't happen to be Michelle, would it?"

With my elbows on my desk, I rest my face in the palm of my right hand, "Rosie, she slept with another man."

Looking like her eyes are going to pop out of her head, "while you were married?"

"No. She just did this."

"And you're upset about her moving on with her life?"

Staring up at her, "it wasn't supposed to happen like that. I decided that I wanted her back."

Laughing out loud, "young man you have a lot to learn." With her hand on her hip, "so how do you think she felt when you were cheating on her, while you were married, with that trifling heifer Felecia? And what do you mean you decided? You messed up. You don't get to decide."

"I know I made a mistake and I've already apologized to her too many times to count."

"And she's supposed to stop her life now that you've acknowledged you made a mistake?"

"I didn't ask her to stop her life. I just wanted her to let me back in."

"I know you Ronald. I watched you mistreat that young lady for years. So now, you find out that someone else is enjoying that sweet nectar and it's driving you crazy, isn't it?"

Is this sweet Rosie talking to me like this? "It sure as hell doesn't feel good. I'm pissed at her because I already told her that I don't share."

"Share what? Her body?"

"Rosie, you don't understand."

"Oh, I understand perfectly well. If you really love Michelle, and not because she's with someone else, then you've got to do more than state your demands. You need to speak with your actions."

"I hear you Rosie. It's... there's something that has been bugging the hell out of me about this whole ordeal. When I went over to her house, she was upset over sleeping with this guy..."

Interrupting me, "he didn't rape her, did he?"

Frowning at her, "no and stop being so dramatic." Shaking my head, "anyways, she said that she doesn't have random sex and that she gave a part of herself that she can never get back."

"Ronnie, your ex is a young lady with strong morals. What she was telling you is that she had sex with a man that she doesn't love. If she was crying, it's because she still loves you. She probably won't admit it, but that's exactly what it sounds like to me."

"Do you really think she loves me?"

"Do you love her?"

"More than anything."

"Then you need to look past the fact that she slept with someone else and stop acting as if she betrayed you. You betrayed her. Can you look past what she's done and forgive her? And before you answer that, I want to remind you that she didn't cheat on you. You're divorced."

"In time, I know I can." Leaning back in my chair, "I'm not going to lie, it hurts like hell. I love her so much Rosie. I'll do anything to get her back."

Coming around the desk to pat me on the shoulder, "you're a good man, Ronald. You're a little too cocky though." Holding up her hands, "now, I'm not trying to put you down, but you need to hear this. If you want Michelle back, you need to humble yourself." Jabbing me in the chest with her pointing finger, "we all make mistakes. As the Bible says, *we reap what we sow*. It's in all things Ronnie, good and bad. Some of the pain you're feeling is the reaping what you've sown process. If you think you're hurting right now, imagine how you've hurt her." Leaning down to hug me, "humble yourself and work on getting your wife back."

Getting up from my desk to hug her, "thank you Rosie. I can always count on you to tell me like it is."

Chapter Twenty Six

"Ms. Barnett, I have a Ronnie Wen on the phone for you." Amanda says over the intercom.

I'm just returning from a site with a potential customer who worked the hell out of my nerves and the last thing I need is to have to deal with Ronnie. "Thanks Amanda, you can put him through." Coming to take a seat behind my desk, "yes, Ronnie."

"Am I catching you at a bad time?"

Hmm, he's sounding all happy. I would have thought he'd still be pouting over me sleeping with Malcolm. Shaking my head, "no, not really. I just got back from a site with an asshole from hell."

"Well, that makes two of us. I just got finished meeting with a jackass from the same neighborhood."

Smiling for the first time today, "maybe they're related."

"That's a possibility," he says, laughing into the phone. "I'm not going to hold you long because I know you're busy. I just wanted to call and let you know that I'm thinking about you."

Thinking about me. Why? "Okay, thanks for calling me."

"You're most welcome. Enjoy the rest of your day."

What in the hell is up with him, "okay, bye."

"Bye beautiful."

Hanging up the phone. How weird is that. Hearing a knock on my door as Amanda pokes her head inside, "Ms. Barnett, these just came for you." Looking at the most beautiful arrangement of yellow roses with red tips. I wonder who sent me roses.

"Are you sure that those are for me?"

Smiling at me with a toothy grin, "oh, they're for you." Giving me the arrangement, "the card says so."

"Wow!" These roses are gorgeous. Pulling the card from the holder as Amanda's walking out of my office, I lean against my desk...

Just because I'm thinking about you.
Love, Ronnie

With my eyebrows raised, what a surprise. He's never sent me just because roses before. Leaning down to smell, they are absolutely beautiful.

Going back to finish up some reports before leaving for the day, I can't wait to get home. After crying on Yolanda's shoulders, she decided to come for a visit. I haven't seen her in almost a year, so we have some major damage to do at the mall.

"Excuse me Ms. Barnett, but there's a Malcolm Stuart on the phone for you."

"Put him through." What in the hell does he want? "Hi Malcolm."

"Hey Shell, I'm not going to hold you long, I wanted to know if you wouldn't mind stopping by after work today?"

"Michelle. What's up with the nickname?"

"What's up with you being so moody?"

"I'm not being moody, I don't like being called *Shell*."

"Stop frowning, because I know you are and for the record, you are being moody."

Whatever! "Well in that case Malc, what time are you going to be home?"

Laughing into the phone, "seeing that I'm the boss, I decided to work from home today."

Smiling, "must be nice."

"Very."

Looking at my watch, "I'm actually going to be leaving here in a few minutes for a hair appointment."

"What time is your hair appointment?"

"At five. Why?"

"I need to talk to you about something important." Hesitating, "do you think you could stop by before your appointment? It's two o'clock now so you'll have plenty of time."

"Yeah, sure. Is something wrong?"

"Nah, just want to talk to you."

"Okay. I get the feeling that something's wrong."

"Nah. I'll see you when you get here."

Hanging up the phone, I take a deep breath. Normally, Malcolm doesn't beat around the bush. Leaning back in my chair with my head against the headrest, maybe he wants to know why I've been avoiding him like the plague since the other night.

I've had many really good orgasms before with Ronnie. But Malcolm, he had my body vibrating for long after it was over. Closing my eyes, and the way he was moving, um. Crossing my legs, Yolanda was right when she said that having a taste of something else lets you know if what you've gotten before is the real thing. The problem with that is, I still feel a bit disgusted with myself. As good as it was, I felt so unfulfilled and disconnected afterwards.

Taking time to think and completely process my thoughts, I've come to the conclusion that the reason I didn't feel that way after having sex with Ronnie is because although I'm not in love with him, I do have strong feelings for him.

I almost wish that Malcolm would tell me that he's decided to move on so that I can stop feeling guilty about the direction of our relationship. He deserves more than I'm willing to give and I really don't have a legitimate reason to break it off with him other than being emotionally stupid.

Getting up from my desk, I grab my purse to leave. Thank you Lord for clarity in my thoughts.

Arriving at Malcolm's house, I have butterflies in my stomach.

Coming from around the back of his house, he's dressed in sweats and a long sleeved shirt. "Hey lady."

"Breaking out the fall clothes already?"

Pulling me into a hug, "it's my favorite time of the year." Following him into the house, "want something to drink?"

Walking into the kitchen, I can't even look at his island. Taking a seat at the table, "no, I'm good."

Staring at me with a smirk on his face, "you don't want to join me here at the island?"

Trying to contain my smile, "I'm good here."

Rubbing his hand across the island, "you were good here too." Cracking up laughing, "I'm sorry. You have to admit, you walked right into that one. Plus, you're cute when you blush."

"What do you want to talk about?" I'm asking, trying to change the subject.

"Are you comfortable in here?"

"Can you just get to the point? And while you're over there laughing, did you at least clean it off."

"You mean this island?" He says, rubbing his hand across the surface again. "After it lost your scent, I did."

What the hell!

Laughing while holding up his hands, "okay. Okay. I'm sorry. I see that you're not in the joking mood."

Rolling my eyes at him, "can you just get to the point?"

Grabbing my hand, "let's talk in the den." Turning off the television, he sits down beside me on the sofa. "The reason I asked you to come over is to get your feelings on something that's come up."

"Is it something serious?"

"Not really. Well, maybe it is."

"Can you just spit it out?"

Leaning forward with his elbows resting on his knees, "Michelle, you mean the world to me." Looking back at me, "last week, I got a call from Angie, a young lady who I dated in college." Biting the side of his lip, "she's going to be in town on Sunday and I'd really like to spend some time with her." Using his hands, "I can't do that with a good conscience if I'm not honest with you."

Wow! Where did this man come from and what in the hell is wrong with me that I don't love him instead? Looking at him, "I guess I don't get what you're asking me."

"How do you feel about me seeing her?"

"I honestly don't know. I think I'm shocked that you asked."

"It's important to me that you're okay with this."

Is he breaking up with me? I think he's trying to without hurting my feelings. "Malcolm, I want you to be happy. If you're trying to break up with me then just say it." I'm saying, with a smile on my face, while playfully punching him in the arm.

Smiling as he releases his breath, "I am breaking up with you, but with your permission."

Moving to sit closer to him, "I'm sorry that I can't give you what you deserve. And if Angie can, then you have my blessings as long as we can remain friends." I say holding up my pinky finger.

"Deal, but I'm not doing no pinky swear."

"Why not, it seals the deal."

"Cause, I'm a man and men don't pinky swear." Pulling me into a hug, "however, I can think of another way to seal the deal in the kitchen."

Hugging him back, "no way. Besides, you have a woman now."

"I don't have her yet. There was someone special taking up residence in my heart. I'll work on getting her on Sunday." Letting me go, "thank you Michelle."

"You're welcome. Well, I better get going."

"Okay, and I mean it Michelle, we're friends. No one can come between us."

"I'll only agree if you pinky swear."

"Give me your damn finger!"

Getting into my car, I look towards the heavens. Thank you Jesus for answering my prayers.

Chapter Twenty Seven

It's a week before Thanksgiving and I've been contemplating whether or not I should ask Michelle if she wants to go with me to my parents for dinner.

The entire time we were married, she spent the holidays with me and my parents or stayed home alone with the exception of the one or two times I remember her going to her dad's house. The thought of her being alone this year bothers me.

I'm trying to take Rosie's advice by humbling myself which is hard as hell when having to deal with Michelle. I didn't realize how bossy I was in our relationship until now. All this, *'can we do this or would you like to do that'* crap is for the birds. I guess I'm more like Aiden than I realized.

Might as well make the call...

"Hello." She answers the phone sounding all out of breath.

"Michelle. I'm not disturbing you am I?"

"No, just got off the treadmill."

Leaning back against the sofa, "treadmill?" Michelle only gets on the treadmill when she's trying to analyze her thoughts — at least that's what she's always said.

"Yeah. I'm trying to make a decision on a possible job opportunity and it's really stressing me out."

"Really, I didn't know you were considering leaving Brockman and Goldstein."

Exhaling her breath, "right now it's just a thought. I don't know if you remember Todd? He used to work at the firm."

Rolling my eyes, I remember his ass from the club. "The guy at the club?"

Laughing into the phone. "Um hmm."

"What's funny?"

"You. And the way you said, *the guy at the club.*"

"On with your problem, Michelle."

Laughing again, "well anyways, *Todd* has this idea that we should start our own business."

"Just you and him?"

"No, there's five of us. Two architects, Todd and Felton; two engineers, me and Daniel and then there's Jason, he's going to handle the business side of the deal, which is the financial and marketing stuff."

"Sounds like a good idea."

"It's a really good idea and the proposal is impressive. I'm just not sure about the individual financial investment that's required to get started."

"Is money the only problem you have with the proposal?"

"That among the instability of getting involved in a venture like this. I trust Todd and I know that what he has in mind is promising. But, with anything new, there's going to be hiccups. I guess, I'm worried about the hiccups."

"I can understand your concern. If you don't mind me asking, how much money are each of you required to invest?"

Loudly sighing into the phone, "thirty thousand dollars."

"That's a lot of money. Then again, in order to be successful, you have to take some risks."

"I know that. But, am I willing to take such a loss if we're not successful."

Choosing how I should say this to her, because she's probably going to go off on me for getting into her business, "do you have the money to invest because if you don't, I can give it to you."

Hesitating to answer, "I have the money. Thanks for offering."

Wow. Progress. "I'm sure you've dissected that proposal a million times but sometimes Michelle, we have to be willing to take risks. Some success comes out of risks."

"Yeah, you're right." She says, sighing into the phone. "If I decide to go along with them, I think I'm going to continue to work at the firm, just in case. That's part of the problem too. Todd feels that if we're still working that we can't give 100%. I don't necessarily agree with him because he hasn't taken into consideration that we're all single. If this fails, he has his wife to take up his slack."

Offended. "And you have me."

"No. I have myself."

"I didn't mean it like that."

"Then how did you mean it? You know what, never mind. This is something I have to figure out for myself."

"Never mind? I mind. Why would you say some shit like that?"

"Don't cuss at me. Why wouldn't I say what I said? Every time I try and have a civilized conversation with you, you have to ruin it by saying something crazy."

"Not as crazy as you fucking some other dude!"

"What! I know you didn't just say that!"

Abruptly getting up from the sofa, "yes hell, I said it. I'm still mad at your ass for that shit too!"

"I don't give a good damn about you being mad!"

"That's obvious. I told your ass that I don't share anything. Especially, not my pussy."

"It's not your pussy! Oh...but, you didn't have a problem sharing *my dick* with that bitch Felecia. Did you? You were paying that hoes rent and you tripping because I slept with Malcolm. Please."

"Stop bringing up past shit. And my fucking her is different from you fucking that son of a bitch!"

"How is it different?" Before he can answer. "Yeah asshole, that's what I thought. The only difference is, when you were fucking her, we were married."

"I know damn well you didn't just call me an asshole."

"Yeah, I did and I'm not going to apologize for saying it either. I do one thing and you act like it's the end of the world. So what, I hurt your feelings by fucking Malcolm. How many times did you hurt my feelings when you were fucking that bitch?"

This argument has gotten way out of control. Damn. I shouldn't have said all this shit to her. Talking, my voice barely above a whisper, "Michelle, I'm sorry. I didn't mean to take our conversation there. Since were talking, if what you felt when I was fooling around with Felecia feels anything like what I felt when I found out about Malcolm, I'm sorry. I don't think I've had anything, with the exception of our divorce, to hurt me so badly."

"I'll talk to you later, Ronnie."

"Okay. But before you hang up, I wanted to know if you want to spend Thanksgiving with me?"

"No and thanks for asking."

Hanging up the phone, why did I say that shit to her? Sitting back down on the sofa, maybe I just needed to get it off my chest. I'll make it up to her in a few days.

Chapter Twenty Eight

"Why didn't you tell me that you were spending Thanksgiving by yourself?" Yolanda is asking over the phone.

"It's just a day. I'm thankful and I don't mind being alone."

"I know, but I still wish you would have said something."

Changing the subject, "so are you nervous about meeting Daren's parents?"

"Hell yes. That's why you should have told me that you were spending the holiday alone."

Hearing the doorbell, I'm getting up from the floor in my office, heading downstairs to see who it is. "I don't recall you ever going to meet 'the parents' during any holiday."

"I have, once or twice. This time is different because I'm really feeling Daren. He's a good guy."

"I'm happy for you. Hold on a sec." Looking through the peephole, it's Ronnie. "Yolanda, call me later." Opening the door, "yeah. Call me later."

Holding up bags, "I brought peace offerings."

Smirking, "Why aren't you at your parents?"

"Because, I want to be here with you." Shifting the bags in his hands, "are you going to let me in or what?"

Standing back so that he can enter, I follow him into the kitchen. "You just assumed I didn't cook."

Glancing over his shoulder, "Oh, I know you didn't cook."

Walking over to lean against the counter, "don't act like I don't know how to cook." Looking into one of the shopping bags, "what all did you buy?"

"Everything. I'll be back."

"There's more?"

"Yep. I'll be back."

Returning with a few pots, "Ronnie, I do own pots and pans."

"I wasn't sure, so I came prepared."

Helping him take the food out of the bags, I walk around to the opposite side of the island to where he's standing to hug him. Turning so that he can hug me back, "thanks Ronnie. You really didn't have to do this. I really do appreciate it."

"I know and I wanted to."

Finally releasing his hold, I return to helping him. "That's a big turkey for two people."

Laughing, he looks over at me. "It was the only one left in the store. I started to get chicken."

"Do you even know how to bake a turkey?"

"It can't be too hard. A turkey is nothing more than an oversized chicken."

Rolling my eyes in his direction, "you are so silly." Laying my hand on my chest, "believe it or not, I know how to bake a turkey."

Running water over the turkey, "since when?"

Going to stand next to him, "since my grandmother taught me how to do it. And stop looking at me like that. I know how to cook a turkey."

Leaning over to kiss me on the nose, "if you say so."

"Fine. Don't believe me. What can I do?"

"I don't know. We're having turkey, dressing, green beans, corn and rolls. Choose what you can cook."

"You act like I've never cooked for you before."

"I didn't say that but you have to admit, I always did most of the cooking when we were married."

Pulling out a bowl from underneath the counter for him to mix the ingredients for the dressing, "only because you got home first. Anyways, I don't have to prove anything to you. I can cook."

"You are too cute when you pout."

Not responding, I help to prepare the other items. "Know what we need?"

"I have no idea. What do we need?"

"Dessert. I'll be back."

Chapter Twenty Nine

Michelle has the ideal kitchen. This kitchen is nicer than some of the kitchens that I've seen in new homes.

Adjusting the temperature on the oven, I put the turkey inside.

I had a blast joking with her about her cooking skills. I know she can cook. And she's right, when we were married, I did most of the cooking because I usually got home first.

Hearing her home phone ringing, the machine comes on.

Hey Michelle. Just calling to wish you a Happy Thanksgiving. Call me.

"Now I'm going to show you that I can cook." She says, walking into the kitchen.

"Thought you said you don't have anything to prove to me."

"I don't." Placing the items on the counter top that she purchased for the sweet potato pie, she opens a drawer and pulls out a cookbook.

Watching her work is so damn erotic. She's wearing black stretch pants and blouse that's hugging her body like a glove. Leaning against the island with my ankles crossed and my arms folded, "Michelle, now I'm not trying to start an argument, but why did you wear that to the store."

Placing the potato back on the counter, "you're doing it again."

Holding up my hands, "I know. I know. It's just that." Shaking my head, "never mind."

Turning back to peel the potatoes, she places them inside a pot to boil. Wiping her hands, she turns to look at me, "want to watch a movie while we wait?"

"No mushy stuff."

"For your information, I don't watch mushy stuff. I like action too." She says bending over to pull some movies out for us to watch.

Sitting down on the sofa trying to adjust my growing erection, "I want hard core action." Oh damn, hard core makes me think of sex and watching her bending over like that reminds how long it's been since I last had sex.

"You okay?" She's asking, with a frown on her face as she's walking towards me.

"I'm fine."

"You look like you're in pain." Sitting down on the sofa, she turns sideways with her leg bent facing me, "this is what I have. What do you want to watch?"

Sorting through the movies, I pick up 'Crank.' What the hell? "Have you seen this movie?"

Taking the movie from me she smiles, "yeah, I've seen it. This is Malcolm's movie."

What the hell is she smiling about? Rubbing my hands against my jeans, "Malcolm's, huh?"

Taking the movie from her hand, I lay it on the sofa table. I wonder if that's what they watched when she gave up my goodies. "I don't want to watch that. What else do you have that belongs to you?"

With her head down, she glances up at me, "this is all I have unless you want to order something on pay per view." Getting up from the sofa, she goes into the kitchen. "Oh," she says coming back into the room. "I have some movies in my bedroom. I'll get those."

Lord, please don't let this girl come back in here with another movie like 'Crank.' Leaning back against the sofa, I close my eyes. I wonder where they had sex. Was it here or at his place? If here, which room?

"I found these and I think this one belongs to you." She says, holding up 'Die Hard.'

"I was looking for this movie the other night. It was on cable, but I came in at the end of it." Thank you Lord! At least my movie was in her bedroom.

"I take it that's what you want to watch."

"If it's okay with you. I can always watch it at home now that you're finally returning it to me."

"Whatever. I didn't even know I had it." Taking the movie from me, she puts it in the disc player and comes back to take a seat on the sofa.

After laughing through Die Hard and cooking our meal, we decide to watch Bad Boys. Half way through the movie, we place it on hold to make our plates. Following Michelle into the kitchen, "I'm starving."

"Me too. Everything smells so good."

"Yeah, even your pie."

Looking at me, "ha, ha. I'm going to love watching you lick your fingers."

"Michelle, you do remember that we were once married, right?"

"No Ronnie, I totally forgot."

"Drop the sarcasm. What I'm saying is, you know what turns me on. I'm a man attracted to his wife." Looking at her expression, "sorry, ex-wife, be mindful of what you say."

Shaking her head, "I'll keep that in mind."

Making our plates, "do you mind if we eat our dinner while watching the movie."

"No, I don't mind."

"Here," holding out my hand, "give me your plate and you get the drinks."

Going back to watch the movie, "I hate to admit this, but your turkey is pretty good."

Smirking at her, "and your corn and green beans are good too."

Throwing a corn kernel at me, "don't be funny. Who can mess up canned food?"

"You'd be surprised. Hey, what time is it?"

Looking at her cell phone, "it's 3:30." Before she can place it back on the table, it rings. "Hello."

Glancing in my direction, "yeah, I'm good." Smiling, "no, I decided to stay home. Where's Angie?" Laughing, "I'm glad you're having fun. Okay. Call me later. Bye."

"By the way, Malcolm called while you were gone to the store."

"That's what he just told me."

"So you two aren't dating anymore?"

Staring at the television, "no, not anymore."

Yes! Thank you Jesus! Trying to sound concerned, which I'm definitely not. "What happened?"

"Don't even try it."

Laughing at her, "you don't seem too upset over it."

"I'm not. Malcolm is a good man and he deserves someone who really wants to be with him."

Maybe Rosie really does knows what she's talking about. "Well, I'm happy for him. Anyways, you know I have to watch the game."

"I know. Are you done with your plate?"

"Yeah, I got it. Hey, what happened with the business proposal you were telling me about last week."

Opening the dishwasher, she rinses off her plate while holding out her hand for mine. "We had an argument over this very subject last week so I don't want to talk about it."

"I said I was sorry. Tell me about it." Grabbing her hand, "Michelle, I'm really interested."

Exhaling a breath, she smiles. "The proposal is upstairs. I'll go get it so you can see it for yourself."

Going back into her family room to wait for her, she comes back and sits down next to me, extremely close, with her knees bent and her feet propped up on the sofa. Passing me the proposal, it looks really impressive. And like I already knew she would, it's dissected from the first page to the last. "*Designs of Stone,* hmm."

"I'm really considering maybe making the investment. I listened to what you said about taking the risk and honestly, I have nothing to lose." Pinching her bottom lip, "the only thing that's still holding me back is losing my health insurance benefits. I mean, I can pay for COBRA until we're up and running. It's just so expensive."

Turning the page of the proposal, "you wouldn't have to quit right away though, would you?"

"Not right away, but within the next six months. Which means I would have to give my notice in the next four months."

"Four months. You have to give them a four month notice?"

"For junior partners, it's requested, not really required. I'm trying not to burn any bridges."

"Yeah, that's law." I respond. "I still have you on my health insurance."

Frowning at me, "Why would you still have me on your insurance?"

"I never got around to changing it." Raising my head up from the report, we're looking each other in the eyes. Hearing the hitch in her voice, she slowly looks away.

"You should probably have it cancelled."

Placing my hand on top of her knees, she looks at me again, "Michelle, you want me to cut all ties from you and I can't. I couldn't even if I wanted to."

Biting the inside of her left lip, something she's always done whenever thinking too much, "that makes you responsible for me and you're not. You're not responsible for me anymore."

With the proposal in my left hand, I turn to face her while wrapping my arms around her shoulder, "In my mind, I'm always going to be responsible for you. I love you so much. I know I've hurt you in the past and like I said before, I was wrong. I regret so much for not appreciating you when we were married. Let me do this for you. Don't let not having health insurance be the reason that you don't get involved in this." Holding up the proposal, "this is a solid opportunity."

Biting the inside of her lip, I lean forward covering the distance between us to kiss her. Pulling back, "I'll think about it." She says, her voice just above a whisper. "I'll bet the game is getting ready to start."

Removing my arm, "yeah, I think it is." Eyes still locked to hers, "I'm going to try some of that sweet potato pie before kickoff."

Nodding her head, she takes the proposal from me and heads upstairs while I'm going into the kitchen.

Chapter Thirty

Squinting my eyes at the light coming from the television, Ronnie's lying on top of me. In between my legs to be exact and he's heavy. Arching my back to try and get comfortable, "Ronnie. Ronnie. Get up."

Turning his head, his face brushes against my breast. "Hmm, what's wrong?"

"You're heavy. Get up."

Pulling his hand up to squeeze my hip, he rubs his face against my breast again. Placing my hand on top of his, "Ronnie, get up."

"Okay." He says, in a sleep groggy voice.

Waiting for him to get up, his weight feels so good, yet I can't give into him.

"You feel so damn good. Hmm," he says, grinding his hips into the sofa. "If only this sofa were you."

"Ronnie, get up." I'm saying, as I'm trying to shift my body to get him to move.

Raising up, "what time is it."

"I don't know." Sitting up and moving back against the arm of the sofa, I grab my phone. "It's two in the morning." Rubbing my hand through my hair, "what time did I fall asleep?"

"I think it was around the third quarter."

"Who won?"

"I have no idea. After about the second slice of your pie," smiling that sexy smile that used to make me drop my panties, "which was actually pretty good, I fell asleep."

Getting up from the sofa, "told you it was going to be good."

Staring at me, "it was good. Do I have to leave?"

Rubbing against the hair at my temple, "I don't think we should be having sex. If you stay, that's what will more than likely happen."

"What if I promise to just hold you?"

"I don't know..."

Getting up from the sofa and coming to stand in front of me with his hands on my waist, "we can sleep with our clothes on. Please, babe. I need to hold you." Moving his hands up to cup my face, "I promise, I won't do anything you don't want me to."

"Yeah, well, it's not wise to play with temptation. You can stay, but only if you sleep upstairs." Pulling away from him, I go into my bedroom and lock the door.

"You don't have to lock your door, I'll be upstairs." He says, tapping on my door.

Yes hell I do need to lock my door. It will remind me that I don't need to indulge in the temptation upstairs.

Chapter Thirty One
Three months later...

Today is Valentine's Day and I have something special planned for Michelle. Hopefully, she'll like it so much that she'll finally give in and give me some. I swear, when she makes up in her mind that she's going to stick to something, she does. I've tried every trick in the book to get that booty, nothing works. Glancing down at the time on my computer, I need to see if things are going as planned...

"Brockman and Goldstein, this is Shelby, how may I help you?"

"Yes, can I speak to Michelle Wen, I mean Michelle Barnett?" Damn, did I just slip like that?

"May I ask whose calling?"

"Ronald Wen."

"Please hold."

"This is Michelle."

"Hi beautiful. How's your day going?"

Hearing her smiling into the phone, "my day is going quite well. Thank you for the roses and teddy bear."

"You're welcome. Do you like your teddy bear?"

"Yes Ronnie, I love the bear. Can you tell me how I'm going to get him inside my car?"

Laughing out loud, "I may have to come by and get him for you." The bear that I purchased for her is huge. Feeling that I needed to go over the top for this day, it was a done deal. I had to buy it. "Did you read the card?"

"Um hmm."

"So, what's your answer?"

"Why can't you pick me up?"

"Because, for what I have planned, you need to do what the card says."

"Hold on a sec, Ronnie." She's talking to someone in her office. "Okay, I'm back."

"Like I was saying, you need to do what the card says and nowhere on that card does it mention you going home."

"It also doesn't mention sex, but I know it's a part of your plan."

This girl. I'm going to develop blue balls dealing with her ass. "Listen babe, please come over. Follow the instructions on the card and I promise, you won't regret it."

Sighing into the phone, "I'll do it. I have a hair appointment scheduled for today, so I may be a little late."

"You may need to change your hair appointment to Saturday."

"Why?"

Cracking up at my wild thoughts, "no reason. I'll see you this evening. Hey, can't you get an earlier appointment for your hair?"

"No, I can't. And if you think you're going to mess up my hair, forget it. I know why you were laughing."

"Can't blame a horny man for trying."

Laughing at my comment, "thanks again for the gifts. I'll see you this evening."

Stepping out of the shower, I have a special evening prepared for Michelle. When we dated back in college, I used to go overboard for her on all holidays and somewhere along the way I didn't feel it necessary to do those things for her anymore. I realize that trying to get someone to forgive and trust again isn't easy. Sometimes, I really wonder if she'll ever get there. She gives just a little and then she pulls back. I keep thinking that if I keep telling her that I love her, keep being there for her, keep doing the little things that make her smile that eventually, she'll believe in me again.

Hearing the chime of the alarm, she's finally here. The note from this afternoon ended with her meeting me here at the house. Now the fun begins. There are more notes all over the house leading her from one room to the next. I'm estimating that she's in our bedroom now. There, I have instructions for her to get undressed and soak in the tub that I have prepared for her. The only light is from the many candles that I have placed around the bathroom. With her favorite J'adore fragrance and jazz playing throughout the house, I'm hoping to set the desired mood.

After her bath, there are instructions for her to go into our walk in closet to retrieve the wrapped box that I left on the island. I can just see her debating in her mind whether or not she should wear what I've purchased for her. Hearing the clicking of her heels against the tile, I have my answer. Standing at the far side of the room as she enters, the expression on her face is priceless. It took me two hours to clear out this room, but she's so worth it. The floor is completely covered with red and white rose petals. In the middle of the room is a blanket with a picnic basket filled with pineapples, strawberries and cheese. Holding a glass of red wine in my hand, "Happy Valentine's Day baby."

Clearly taking a few minutes to compose herself, "Ronnie, you didn't have to do all of this. It', it's really beautiful."

"Not as beautiful as you are." Taking in the red silk robe that stops at her thighs and the black, red bottom heels, I feel like I'm going to combust. "I wanted to do this for you." Walking over to pull her into the room, I turn my head just enough to capture her lips into the kiss that I've been craving all day. Trying to control myself, I'm hoping like hell that she'll let me see the bra and panties that I bought for her.

"When did you have time to do all of this?"

Damn, I'm horny. "I hope you like it?"

Following me into the room, "I love it." She says, sitting down on the blanket.

"Why do you sound so shocked?"

"No reason. Well actually, this is a lot. You've never done anything like this before."

Staring at her, "your hair is beautiful, by the way."

"Oh, here's your gift." Handing me a gold bag with black paper sticking out of it, "if I had known you were going to do all of this, I would have put more thought into my purchase."

"Valentine's Day isn't for men. But, there is one gift that you can give me that would be very thoughtful."

"What's that?" Looking at me, "no! I already told you, I'm not messing up my hair."

That's what you think. Leaning my head to the side, "how do you know that's what I'm talking about?"

Eating a strawberry from tray, "because I know you."

"Can't I at least get a peek at the bra and panties?"

Smirking at me, "I'll think about it."

Leaning forward, I kiss her on the lips. "How long is it going to take for you to think about it?"

Kissing me back. "I don't know, you have to be patient."

"I have been patient. So how long is it going to take for you to think about it?" Running my hand up her leg, stopping at her thigh, "I just want to see you."

"Me or the lingerie?"

"Both."

"If I let you see, is that all you want to do?"

Trailing kisses from her lips to her neck, "no, I want more. But, I'll settle for a peek."

"Just a peek, okay."

Pulling at the knot in her robe, "okay." Untying the knot, I take my finger to open her robe. Damn! "Babe, you look good."

"Thank you." Placing her hand on top of mine, "just a peek, no touching."

"You're killing me. You know that don't you."

"I won't let you die."

"You sure?" Nodding at me, her eyes are so sexy. "I have another gift for you?"

Smiling at me, "don't you think you've already given me enough?"

"No. I don't." Taking a deep breath, "you know Michelle, I started wearing my wedding band about a month ago and you haven't said anything about it even though I know you've noticed." Seeing the look on her face, "I'm not suggesting that you wear your ring. It's just, I've been thinking about what a ring symbolizes. I realize that it's a promise between two people who love each other."

Holding up her hands, "Ronnie, don't..."

"Let me finish." Reaching into my pocket, I pull out the blue Tiffany's box. "I don't want to try and rush you into anything but this ring," taking it out of the box, "symbolizes my love for you. I love you and I regret that I ever messed up our marriage. The pregnancy before was just as much my fault as it was yours. I was stupid to try and place all the blame on you. And my cheating, that was wrong too." Wiping the tears from my eyes that have managed to escape, "this ring isn't much, but it says what I feel."

Biting her bottom lip, left side, she's looking at me like she wants to burst into tears. "Ronnie, this is a beautiful ring. I just can't accept it."

The ring is a platinum band of hearts. There are three rows total. The two rows on the outside have platinum hearts and the row on the inside is covered in heart shaped diamonds. The center has a one carat heart shaped diamond also surrounded by smaller diamonds.

Taking her right hand, "yes, you can. Please. You can wear it on your right hand. It's nothing more than a promise ring. It's my promise to you that I'm going to be faithful. I'm going to love you. I'm going to express my love for you in private and in public. I'm going to take care of you..."

"Ronnie, please stop. This is too much. This ring, your words, it's all too much."

"Do you love me?"

Looking away, "I can't answer that."

"Yes, you can. You just choose not to. I know you love me. Without ever hearing the words coming from your mouth, I know you love me." Wiping my tears away, "do you trust me?"

Looking down at her hands, "I'm afraid to trust you."

Pulling her chin up so that she'll look at me, "I know you're afraid. I'm afraid too. I'm afraid that after all I do, I'll never earn your complete trust. But, I'm not going to give up. I can't. You mean too much to me. Don't you know that? Can't you see how much you mean to me?"

Chapter Thirty Two

Looking down at this ring in his hand, it's absolutely beautiful. I just can't accept it. He's making promises to me that I'm not sure if I can reciprocate. What's freaking me out is the fact that I've never seen this side of him before. Ever.

"Ronnie, you seem to be so sure about what you want and I don't know if it's what I want. If I accept this ring, you might feel that I'm sending you a message that I'm not trying to send. We need to be clear with each other."

Clearing his throat, there is so much emotion in his voice, "you've been clear with me. But, I need you to realize that I'm not letting you go again. I love you. And whether you want to admit it or not, you still love me too. I can tell by the way that you look at me when you think I'm not paying attention. I hear it in your voice sometimes over the phone. I see it in your body language. I know you love me."

He's exaggerating, nothing about my actions have said that I love him. Releasing a frustrated breath, "why are you making things so complicated?

You can't up and spring stuff on me like this. A ring? Look, I have to have time to process things and you never want to give me time to do that. You just keep throwing me off and I can't think straight when you do that and you know it."

"Baby, I'm not trying to complicate things. This ring isn't for you, it's for me." Holding the ring up, "you wearing this ring will remind me of my promise to you."

Staring at him, "Ronnie, that makes no sense at all and you know it."

Laughing, "I may not be wording it the right way, but it makes perfect of sense to me." Looking into my eyes, "please Michelle. Please wear it for me. I know you're still trying to sort out your feelings for me but baby, I'm being straight with you. I love you and only you. There is no other woman for me. Only you."

"Let me get this straight. You want me to wear this ring, that I know cost maybe five thousand dollars or more, to represent your promise to me?" Nodding his head. "You said earlier that a wedding ring symbolizes a promise of love between two people. Am I right?" Nodding his head, "so technically, a promise ring and a wedding ring is the same thing, right?"

"Stop trying to dissect this Michelle."

"Stop trying to manipulate me."

"Are you not going to wear the ring?"

Shaking my head because I know I'm not going to get anywhere with him at the rate that we're going. "Is this a gift in honor of Valentine's Day or is this your way of trying to manipulate me into doing something you want me to do?"

"Which answer will get you to wear the ring?"

"Definitely, saying it's a gift because I won't be obligated to wear it."

Staring at me for a long time, he grabs my hand and places the ring on my left, middle finger. "You're really going to make me work to be with you, aren't you?" Not responding to him. He leans forward and kisses me on the nose, "I'm up for the challenge." Looking down at his watch, "we better get going or we're going to be late for our reservations."

"Where are we going? Will I have time to go home and change?"

Hitting me on the butt, "it's a surprise and I have everything you need right here."

Looking over my shoulder, "you seem to be full of those tonight."

Laughing, he turns me around and hauls me over his shoulder with my butt in the air, "I'd like to fill you with something else."

Trying to hold on as he's walking down the stairs, "Ronnie, put me down and please, don't drop me." Reaching his bedroom, he throws me down on the bed, landing on top of me. Staring up at him, I have butterflies in my stomach. I want so badly to give in and relieve all this pent up sexual tension, but I know if I start, I won't be able to stop. Ronnie's right, I do love him. I just don't know if I can trust him with my heart again.

Staring down at me, he lets out a silent laugh, "I love you, baby." Getting up from the bed, he pulls me up with him. "Follow me." He says, pulling me inside the closet. Going over to his side of the closet, he grabs a black hanging bag and turns to give it to me. "This what I'd like for you to wear tonight."

Taking the bag from him, I lay it down on the island, unzipping it to see what's inside. Finding a pair of dark denim jeans and a very nice off the shoulder red shirt - all from a very upscale shop here in San Diego. "Wow Ronnie, this is nice." Looking up at him, "you really went all out for this day."

"And it's still not enough."

"What? The roses, the bear, red bottom heels, these clothes, the ring, the lingerie, the room and dinner. That's a lot." Walking around the island that's separating us, I wrap my arms around his neck and give him a peck on the lips, "thank you."

"You're welcome. But you might want to walk back over to the other side because I just had a thought, a very sexual thought, with you spread out on top of this island."

Looking down at the island, it conjures up some memories of another island that I was spread out on. O.M.G! Moving quickly, I grab the bag, "on that note, I'm going to get dressed."

Laughing out loud, "and don't take too long, we have reservations."

In the bathroom getting dressed, I hear Ronnie thanking me for his gift. The day after Thanksgiving, we went shopping. He was looking for a bottle of cologne and not one store that we went into had it. Everyone said it had to be ordered. Then two weeks ago, while in Dallas for a meeting, I found it for him. I didn't realize that it was going to cost almost six hundred dollars. But after all that he's done for me today, he was worth the purchase. "You're welcome." Looking at myself in the mirror, I'm wondering who helped him with picking out this outfit.

Walking out of the bathroom, his slanted eyes are the size of quarters. "Damn, you look good in those jeans!" Handing me the black, pointed toe red bottom heels, "maybe, we should stay in tonight."

Taking the heels from him, "and do what?" Holding up my hand, "forget I asked."

Laughing, "I hope you know I'm getting some tonight." Standing by the door wearing a pair of dark denim jeans, black shirt and jacket, Ronnie is hella fine!

Following him out of the bedroom, "we'll see."

"Shit! You'll see." Smirking at me, "I may be in trouble for letting you wear these jeans tonight."

"Letting me wear these jeans?" Eyes rolled in his direction, "okay, daddy."

Standing in the garage waiting for him to open the car door for me, he pulls me back against his chest while kissing the side of my neck, "daddy huh? Well, daddy really likes you in these jeans and I'm going to love hearing you call me daddy later tonight."

"Me, calling you daddy, while having sex will never happen."

Opening the door, "we'll be making love and you will be calling me daddy. Wait and see, you will."

Getting into the car, "you seem so sure of yourself. Me calling you daddy, is definitely not going to happen. You can count on that."

"Oh, I'm definitely counting on it."

Chapter Thirty Three

It's been a while now since I last talked to Ronnie and 'Cat' is missing him like mad. I knew the moment I met his ass that his package was special. I've had a few men in my life and I must admit, boy is truly blessed. Shit, after a few lessons from me, if he didn't learn nothing else, he damned sure learned how to work the hell of that pole of his. Damn, I miss his ass. I should have kept my mouth closed and instead of going out for dinner tonight, I'd be dinner.

Sitting on my bed to lotion my legs, who am I kidding? Ronnie spent every Valentine's Day with her. *"Nah, I can't be with you today. This day is reserved for my wife."*

Anyways, I'm hanging out with my girls tonight in protest of all the so called lovers. We're going to Two Shades for dinner and jazz. As much as I want to check out Two Shades, its way out of my budget, so I'm glad Karen volunteered to treat me. I just wish she wouldn't have invited Jocelyn. I am not trying to spend my evening playing nice with her because for one, she's never liked me *and* she'still friends with that two faced bitch, Rhonda. *'Girl please, my brother is not going to leave his wife for you. You're nothing more than a side lined ho who got played.'* If it weren't for her, Ronnie and I would still be together. He was the one who said he wanted a divorce. I just helped to speed up the process.

Arriving to the restaurant, it's packed. They have valet parking but hell, it will cost forty dollars just to utilize their service. Having to park in a lot two restaurants away, I'm literally hiking to my destination.

"Felecia, we're over here." Karen is yelling, as I'm entering the restaurant. All my girls are here. Karen, Alexa, Brittany and of course, Jocelyn. I hate her ass. "They say we have a few minutes to wait before we're seated." Karen says.

"Okay, but do we have to stand right here at the entrance?"

"Yes, we do." Alexa says. "I want to see all the single men when they walk in. I'm looking too good to end my night with you heifers."

Bursting out laughing at Alexa's crazy behind, "oh my God! Felecia, isn't that Ronnie?" Karen is asking, while beating the hell out of my arm.

Looking in the direction of the door, it's him. Dressed in a pair of jeans, a black shirt and a dark jacket. Damn, he looks good. And who is this trick he has with him? Her haircut is off the chain, but I'm waiting for her to turn around so that I can see her face. Something about her is familiar. Unable to take my eyes off of him and the hand he has protectively wrapped around this bitch's ass, I hear Jocelyn cracking up laughing. "What are you laughing at?"

"I'm laughing at your ass." She says, rocking all back, pointing her finger at me. "I know you see who he's with. Yeah bitch! That's his wife, Michelle."

Looking at his left hand that he still has wrapped around that woman's ass, he's wearing his wedding ring. Do I freak out or woman up? Oh God, I think I'm going to freak out. Watching her turn her head to look up at him, he leans forward and kisses her on the lips. "Felecia, do you want to leave?" Karen is asking, as she's rubbing my arm. Wanting to say yes, I can see the smirk on Jocelyn's face.

"No, I'm goo..." Before I can finish my sentence, Jocelyn is headed in their direction. Oh God, please help me. Watching closely, because I can't hear anything, not that I'm not trying, Ronnie hugs her and then introduces that woman who also leans in for a hug.

"Damn, I can't believe Ronnie was cheating on her. She's beautiful." Rolling my eyes at Alexa. She's supposed to be on my side. "Girl check out those red bottom heels. I know she paid about eight hundred dollars for those bad boys."

"No, check out that ring." Brittany says. My so called friends have turned on me.

"Why are y'all tripping over this girl? It's just a ring."

"Bitch please, you don't see that bling?" Alexa says. Before I can say anything, Jocelyn is walking back in our direction with this huge smile on her face. I can't stand her ass! Think she's all that because she's married to a doctor.

Karen is the first to speak when Jocelyn returns, "girl what did he say?"

"He said that he and his beautiful wife, Michelle, are out celebrating Valentine's Day." Staring pointedly at me, "I told you, married men will almost never leave their wives for a side lined ho like you."

Right as I'm about to put her ass in check, our party is called and we're being led to our table, which just so happens to be in direct view of Ronnie. Damn, what a night. Listening to Alexa and Karen talking about some drink they want to try, I look up to find them stopped directly in front of our table. And to add insult to injury, he's standing behind her with his left hand resting on her hip, pretending not to see me. Being seated two tables in front of us, I refuse to go down defeated. "Uh Jocelyn, I know you're going to call Rhonda and tell her about this evening so you make sure you tell her that I don't give a damn."

"Girl please. Your ass is sick with envy and stupidity. You bragged about how you called that man's wife and told her about all the shit that Ronnie was doing for your gold digging ass. Failing to realize that he was treating you like nothing more than a high classed ho. You thought that shit was funny at the time, but it backfired on your ass. Look at who he's with and how he's treating her, while you're sitting over here looking stupid as hell." Nodding her head in their direction, "look at that man all over that girl. He loves her. A blind man can see that shit." Laughing out loud, "he passed by this table and didn't even give your ass half a glance."

I hate this bitch. "Baby please, that's all an act. I know Ronnie. And for your information, he was the one who said he didn't want her ass. He came to me."

Smirking at me over the rim of her wine glass, "you don't get it, do you? Look at that girl, she's beautiful. She's classy. And, she's educated. Ronnie was with her while in college. He married her and all you were from the moment he met you, was a piece of prostituted ass. Don't come up in here trying to front. If you meant anything to him, he would have married you instead of her, no matter the circumstance. I don't know what you're looking at, but from the moment they walked in that door to now," she says, pointing her glass in my direction, "he hasn't taken his hands off of her. And I know you saw that ring on her finger. Bling! Yeah, he bought that for her as a gift."

"She's educated too, so save your talk boo-boo." Karen says. "And, so what if he bought her a ring. It's not on her ring finger."

"It's not on Felicia's finger either." Brittany says, laughing under her breath.

Pointing her glass in Karen's direction, she leans forward, "going to college doesn't make you educated. As far as the ring, it doesn't matter which finger she wears it on, she's wearing it and not your prostituting ass friend over there." Scrunching up her face, "you know what? The only reason I came tonight was because of Alexa and Brittany." Pointing the glass between me and Karen, "I can't stand you two trifling, home wrecking bitches."

Looking at Alexa and Brittany falling all over each other cracking up, I'm pissed. Throwing my napkin on the table, this evening was an absolute waste of my time.

After having to sit through two hours of watching Ronnie drool all over his *wife* while at their table or basically screwing her on the dance floor, I've had enough. Not to mention these three bitches making wise cracks the entire time has gotten on my last damn nerve.

"I'm ready to go." Focusing on Jocelyn and her imps, I didn't notice that Ronnie and Michelle have also vacated their table until were standing outside with them waiting for our cars. Karen is dropping me off at my car and if I don't want to hike, I have no other choice but to wait. Thank God for all the other patrons waiting because it allows me to stand back as far as I can without being seen. I hear him asking her if she's enjoyed her evening so far. She smiles at him and answers with a kiss on his lips. Planting his hand on her ass, he whispers something in her ear that has her shaking her head. Damn, I wish I could have heard what he said. Watching them get into Ronnie's car and drive away, I can officially say that payback is a bitch!

Chapter Thirty Four

Turning over in bed to wrap my arms around Michelle's naked body, I glance over at the clock. Oh shit, it's after eight and she has to work today.

Nudging the space behind her ear with my nose, "babe, you need to wake up. It's after eight."

Using her shoulder to try and push me away, "I thought you set the alarm."

"I did. You must have turned it off."

"I'm tired and my throat hurts."

"Don't go in today. Stay here with me."

Turning onto her back, "I can't. I have to meet with the marketing team at a site today at noon."

Rubbing my hand across her flat stomach, I grab the sheet into a fist, "good, that gives me time to get some more before you leave."

Pushing at my hand, "no way. I'm too tired." Looking over at me as she's sits up in bed, covering herself with the sheet, "aren't you tired?"

Sitting up beside her, "no, I'm horny."

Rubbing her hand through her hair, she lets out a deep breath. Closing her eyes, she lays back down on the bed. "Ronnie, will you wake me up in thirty minutes?"

Smiling down at her, I wore her ass out last night. I made damn sure to erase every thought of Malcolm from her memory bank. "Sure, I'll wake you up."

When we got home from the restaurant, it was a given that she was going to spend the night. Not giving her a chance to back out, I was all over her. By the time we made it to the bed, the only piece of clothing remaining were her panties.

Getting her to call me daddy was hilarious. I waited until she was at the brink of her orgasm and pulled completely out. She was doing everything in her power to get me to finish and as hard as it was, I had her at my mercy.

"Call me daddy and I'll let you cum."

"What? I'm not calling you daddy."

Grinding into her just enough to hear her moan, I pull out again. "Call me daddy and I'll let you cum."

Trying to grab my butt, I catch both of her wrists and pull them over her head, "Ronnie, stop being silly."

Grinding into her again, "not silly, daddy. Call me daddy."

Pulling out so that only the tip remains, she takes her left heel to try and hold me down. "Ugh Ronnie, stop playing around."

Thrusting back into her, I slowly gyrate my hips until I feel her tightening around me again. Pulling out quickly, "damn, woo, say it baby. Call me daddy."

Throwing her head back, "okay! Damn! Daddy! Are you satisfied?"

Smiling, I use one of my hands to grab the back of her thigh. Pushing it up just enough to give me a different angle of penetration, *"not quite. Who does this pussy belong to?"*

Using her free hand, she's trying to push me off. *"Oh hell no. Get up. Ronnie you play too much. This isn't funny. I'm going to get your ass back for this!"*

Pushing into her, I know she's really close. *"Just tell me that it belongs to me and only me, and I'll let you cum."*

Going deeper, she moans, *"um, Ronnie."*

Pulling out again with only the tip remaining, *"tell me, Michelle. Tell me that this pussy belongs to me. I told you I don't share."*

Frowning, from pleasure and frustration, she hits the bed with her left fist. *"You're acting crazy Ronnie. This isn't funny anymore. You're going too far! Get up. I'm going home."*

Pushing back into her, I want to tell her that she went too far when she fucked that bitch, Malcolm, but I'll keep that to myself. I don't have to say anything. I'm going to show her. Heavily moaning, I pull out again. Leaning down so that my mouth is close to her ear, *"tell daddy that this is my pussy and I'll let you cum. I promise."*

Thrusting back into her, her back arches off the bed. With her head thrown back, she screams, *"it's yours daddy and it belongs to you! Asshole!"*

"That's all daddy wanted to hear, except for the asshole part. I'm going to have to make you pay for that." And I did. All through the night.

Chapter Thirty Five

Trying to move from under the weight of Ronnie's arm and leg, I glance over at the clock. Oh shit! It's ten thirty. Damn, I'm going to be late. "Ronnie, move. You were supposed that wake me up."

Pulling me in tighter into his embrace, "I'm sorry. I guess I fell asleep."

Moving or at least trying to move out of his death grip, "let go. I need to get up."

"Call in today."

Using my shoulder to push him off of me, "Ronnie, come on. I need to get up or I'm going to be really late. I still have to go home and take a shower."

"Take a shower here." He says, rubbing his erect penis against me. "I'm not ready for you to leave yet."

"Ronnie, move. I'm serious. I need to get up."

Reluctantly, he moves his arm and leg, "if you had clothes here, you wouldn't have to drive clear across town to get dressed."

Getting out of his bed, my body is sore. What I really need is a hot bath, not a shower. Looking for my panties, "I don't live here, so why would I have my clothes here?"

Turning onto his back, "don't start that this morning. All I'm saying is that if you're going to be staying the night, it'd be easier if you had something here to wear."

"This was one time. Who says I'm going to be spending the night here?" Stepping into my panties, my thighs are covered in passion marks. Feeling his eyes on me, I look up. "What?"

Shaking his head, "not a damn thing."

"What? It's true. I don't live here."

"Did you have to say it like that? '*I don't live here.*' I know you don't live here. Shit, I'm reminded of it every damn day." Getting out of bed, I follow him out of his bedroom into the living room where I'm sure most of my clothes are.

Not saying anything, because he's obviously having one of his moments, he hands me my shirt and jeans. Walking out of the room, he returns, still naked. Oh my God, this man is fine!

"Where is the site located?"

Rubbing my hand through my hair, which I'm sure shows no evidence of my appointment on yesterday, "it's over on Clarkston, in the arts district." Why won't he put on some clothes or at least underwear?

Smirking at me, he reaches down and grabs his penis, "see, if you had clothes here, daddy could give you a little more loving."

Smirking back at him, I should be mad at his ass for what he did to me. Just thinking about it has me getting wet. "No, I don't think so. I've got to go."

Following me to the door, I turn to give him a hug. Squeezing my butt, he kisses me on the neck, "can I see you later today?"

"We'll see."

Grinding into me, "I'm only going to do this your way for so long Michelle."

"Do what my way?"

"Allow you to call the shots."

Pulling back, call what shots? I should have known that anytime you give Ronnie a foot, he takes a mile. Whatever, I've got to go or I'm going to be late. "I'll talk to you later. If I don't leave now, I'm going to be super late."

Kissing me on the lips, "I'm serious."

Waving from behind, "I'm sure you are. Talk to you later."

Getting onto the highway, thank God there's no traffic. I have got to get in and see my gynecologist before I end up pregnant.

I was so damned turned on last night from all the stuff he was doing and saying that even I was like, damn the condom, just give it to me. And he did. It was so good, my ass was calling him daddy, big daddy and some other stuff I don't know what the hell meant. Exiting the highway, yeah, I need to get on some form of birth control and fast.

Chapter Thirty Six

For the past three weeks, Michelle's been travelling for her job and when not working, she's been meeting with the guys to discuss the plans for their new business venture.

I have to admit, I'm having a really hard time trying to be supportive and understanding because their meetings seem to always interfere on my time with her. Of course, I can't say anything or she'll get upset.

What I can't figure out is how I can feel this way now, and not when we were married. I get so pissed off sometimes when I hear her on the phone talking to them about anything other than business and she seems to do a lot of that with Felton and Jason.

Waiting for her to answer her door, there's a car creeping down the street...

"What are you looking at?"

Leaning in to kiss her, "at a white car that just passed by."

"I think there's an apartment at the end of the block that's available for rent."

"They look suspect. I hope they're not casing the neighborhood."

Glancing back at me with that look that I sometimes hate and at the same time, I sometimes love, "I'm sure that's not the case."

"You don't know that."

"What's wrong with you?"

"Nothing. Why?"

"You're acting all pissed off and moody."

Taking a seat on the sofa, "I'm neither. What gave you that impression?"

"Oh, I don't know...maybe it's that look on your face." Hearing a knock at the door, "that's Jason coming by to pick up some paperwork."

Reaching for the remote, I notice that she's wearing tight jeans and a green, fitted v neck cotton shirt.

"Hey, Jason. Come in. I have the paperwork upstairs."

"What are you up to tonight?" He's asking, following her inside the apartment.

"Not much." She says, entering the living room. "Jason this is Ronnie. Ronnie, this is Jason, my co-worker."

"And soon to be business partner." He says, coming over to shake my hand. "What's up, man?"

'What's up is I'm about to kick your ass for the way you were looking at my wife's ass.' Is what I want to say, but since I can't say that without pissing her off, I simply nod.

Dropping his hand, he glances over at Michelle. "Come on Jason, the paperwork is upstairs."

Following her upstairs, the son of a bitch's eyes are back on my ass. "What time did you get in from Chicago?"

Looking at me out the corner of her eye, "at around four. The rain caused us to have a layover."

"I wonder who the bosses are going to get to travel. Especially, once you and Felton are no longer there?"

"I have no idea. We were talking about that on yesterday." Saying something I can't quite hear, she giggles. "This is my portion of the report and this is the preliminary contract for the Clayton complex that Todd was asking for. I think Felton has the original."

"Has anyone ever told you that you're anal?"

"I am not anal, I'm thorough."

"Thorough and cute."

Coming back down the stairs, "well thanks. You're not so bad yourself."

"Nice to meet you, Ronnie." Ignoring him, "see you later, Michelle. Have a good evening."

"You too, Jason. I'll see you on tomorrow." Closing the door, she has her arms folded across her chest as she's coming to stand in front of me. "What the hell was that?"

"What the hell was what? That bastard was being disrespectful."

"Him trying to shake your hand was disrespectful?"

"No, him trying to shake my hand after I caught him staring at your ass is what was disrespectful. And, why didn't you tell me you were with Felton?"

Glaring at me for longer than necessary, she laughs through her nose. "I'm not going to argue with you over nothing, Ronnie."

"You say it's nothing. Does he know that?"

"Know what?"

"That you're not single. That you have a man."

"What?" She says, frowning with her hand held out. "I don't know why you're acting all jealous. I've known these guys for years. If I had wanted to be with them, believe me, I've had many opportunities to do so. It's not like that with us."

"Jealous? I'm not acting jealous."

"Then what do you call it?" She's asking, with her brows raised.

"It's not jealousy. I know how men think and that bitch..."

"Stop!" She says, holding up her hand. "I'm not doing this with you tonight. If you're trying to argue, you might as well get up and go home or someplace else."

"I'm not trying to argue. I'm stating facts. You walking around here with those tight ass jeans, knowing damn well that fool was coming over and then he comes up in here being all disrespectful and shit...you know what? I'm tripping."

"Yes, you are." She says, crossing her arms.

"Yeah. I am." I respond, getting up to go stand in front of her. "It bothers me that you're spending so much time with these guys, babe. I have a strong dislike for you talking to them about anything other than business and I definitely don't like you wearing these jeans in front of them."

Staring up at me, she shakes her head.

"Why are you looking at me like that? I'm jealous, I admit it."

"Felton and Jason are my friends. Hell, they're more like brothers to me."

Pulling her arms apart, I reach down to pick her up to carry her over to the sofa. Sitting with her straddling my lap, "if you think of Jason as your brother, know your brother's into incest."

Shifting to get comfortable, she giggles. "You are so silly!"

Pulling her chin down so that I can kiss her, "I've missed you." Feeling my growing erection, she looks down. "He missed you too."

"I'm glad you brought *him* up." Moving to get off my lap, I pull her back. "I haven't been able to get in to see my gynecologist which means, Ronnie." She says, poking her finger in my chest, "you have to wear a condom."

"I don't like condoms. I thought you had an appointment last Tuesday."

"I did, but they had to cancel. And the one for this week, I had to cancel."

"I don't like condoms."

"Then you don't want sex because I can't risk getting pregnant."

"Make love. We make love, we don't have sex. Besides, if you get pregnant, it wouldn't be so bad. What? You don't want my baby?"

Moving to get up, "yes, it would be bad. I'm not trying to have a baby."

"When can they get you in for an appointment then?"

"Next Thursday"

"Next Thursday? I'll pull out then."

Staring at me with her brow raised, "uh no. I'm not even going to fall for that." Pushing her off my lap. I get up and grab my keys off the sofa table. "Where are you going?"

"To get some condoms."

Laughing at me, "Ronnie, you really need help."

"I'm going to get plenty when I get back from the store."

Chapter Thirty Seven

"Ronnie, wait. Give me a minute." He has got to be taking medication to keep up this pace. It's two in the morning and we've already had sex, *or made love,* three times and I desperately need to sleep.

"I'm trying to hold you." He says, kissing the back of my neck.

"That's how it starts." Turning onto my back, "don't you ever get tired?"

"We haven't been together in two weeks." He responds, sitting up in bed. "I'll be glad when you're on the pill. I hate wearing these things."

I shouldn't ask this, but I've got to know..."didn't you use condoms when you were having sex with Felecia and the others?"

Turning to glare at me, "why the hell would you ask me some shit like that? Did Malcolm use condoms when you let him fuck you?"

"Yes, he wore *a* condom. I'm only asking because you keep complaining about having to use them with me and if you wore protection when you were sleeping around, if it wasn't a condom, then what did you use?"

"First of all, I only fucked Felecia while we were married, no one else." Getting out of bed, "of course, I wore a condom with that bitch. You're my fucking wife!" He says, pointing at me, "I shouldn't have to use protection when I want to be with you."

"First of all, don't yell at me! Secondly, I am not your wife and thirdly, it was a simple question."

"You don't ask shit like that Michelle. You just don't. That's in the past. I made a mistake and you don't need to keep bringing it up."

"Again, I asked a simple question. And if you feel that way, why do you keep bringing up Malcolm?"

"Because you fucked him, that's why?"

"Because I fucked him. Okay, well does it make you feel better to keep bringing him up?"

Sitting down on the bed with his back to me, "no, Michelle. It doesn't make me feel better. It hurts. It hurts like hell to know that you've been with someone other than me."

"Well I'm sorry that you're hurt Ronnie. I didn't sleep with him to hurt you." Crawling to the end of the bed, "and I wasn't trying to hurt you by bringing up Felecia. At least, it wasn't my intention." Wrapping my arms around his neck. "Will you forgive me?"

"If you give me some more, I will."

Crawling back to the head of the bed, "no, I'm going to sleep."

Tackling me, "not until after I get some."

"No! I'm too tired."

Laughing out loud, "let me hold you then." Pulling me into his chest, "babe, no more bringing up the past. It happened, we can't change it. I want you too much to let anything or anybody stand in my way."

Closing my eyes, "deal. No more bringing up the past."

"Love you."

"Um hmm."

Chapter Thirty Eight

Who is calling her at six in the morning? Pulling out of my hold, she's grabs the phone. Answering, she has her back to me.

"*Hello.*"

"*No, it's okay. What's up?*"

"*Malcolm, it's okay.*"

Malcolm. What the hell does he want?

"*Really?*"

"*That's great.*"

What's great?

"*I don't know. I can try.*"

Pulling the covers over my head, I slide to the foot of the bed and turn her over onto her back. If she's going to talk to him while I'm in bed with her, then I'm not going to make it easy.

"*I'm meeting with the guys after work on Monday to discuss some stuff. Maybe we can get together afterwards?*"

Trying to squeeze her thighs together, I pry them apart while positioning my shoulders between her legs. Licking her clit before sucking it into my mouth, I feel her pushing at my head.

"*No, I'm, I'm okay.* What were you saying?"

"*Um, hmm.*"

"*Yeah.*" She says, in a whisper.

"*Um, hmm.*"

 Lifting off the bed, I'm sucking harder on her clit."

"*Hold, um, on Malcolm.*"

Trying to pull herself out of my hold, "Ronnie, stop." With my arms wrapped underneath her thighs, I lift her so that I can eat her out. "Ah Ronnie, please stop."

"Um, ah, oh!" Picking up the phone, "*Malcolm, I've got to call you back. Bye!*"

Tasting her cum, I quickly move up her body to embed my penis deep inside before her body has time to calm down from her orgasm, without a condom.

"Ronnie, wait. Oh damn! Are you wearing a condom?"

Hell no, and I don't care. Pounding into her, she had no business on the phone talking to him while I'm lying in bed beside her. She better be glad I have a little sense. Any other man would be beating her ass for that shit.

"If you're not, you need to stop. Ah shit!" She moans out. "Get up. I'm serious."

"Just enjoy it. I'll pull out." I'm saying through clenched teeth. Feeling her climax, I cum hard.

"No. You. Didn't!"

Breathing hard, "I'm sorry. I really meant to."

"Get up! Hurry, get up!"

Pulling out of her, "where are you going?"

"I've got to get this out of me." She says, running to the bathroom.

I know I should feel bad, but I don't. "Maybe you're not pregnant. Don't worry about it."

Coming back out of the bathroom, oh shit. I know that look. "Get up and go home. Now! You did this on purpose because I was on the phone with Malcolm."

"What?"

"Don't what me. He was calling to tell me he was engaged. Go home!" She's yelling. "Oh God, I am so stupid! Why do I keep letting this man do this to me?"

"Michelle, calm down."

"No, you've got to go. Don't talk to me again."

Getting out of bed to grab her, "calm down."

"Don't touch me. Just go home. Now!"

"What are you mad about? I didn't wear a condom on Valentine's Day, not once, and you didn't freak out. So sometimes I have to wear a condom and sometimes, I don't? You didn't say anything about me wearing a condom three weeks ago either!"

"That's because I knew I most likely wouldn't get pregnant during those times. You are such an asshole!"

Holding up my hand, "what? What do you mean, you knew?"

"Put your clothes on." She says, yelling at me as she's walking into her closet. "I know my body's rhythm and this is not the time to be having unprotected sex." Coming out of the closet in shorts and a tee shirt, "you know I can't afford to get pregnant right now. But, do you care? No!" She answers for me. "You know I'm going to be quitting my job in the next few months, which means I won't have health insurance."

Pulling on my jeans, "you'll have health insurance." She's so damn dramatic.

Sitting on the bed, "every time I let my guard down just a little bit with you, this is what happens. I can't even tell you that I love you because I don't know what will happen."

"Michelle, stop crying." Dammit! Going to sit next to her, "I should have listened. I was being selfish and I'm sorry."

Looking at me, "you were being an asshole because you heard me on the phone with Malcolm."

Laughing to myself, "I was being an asshole?" Wrapping my arm around her shoulders, "Baby, there are some things you shouldn't do, and talking on the phone to another man, while your man is in the bed is not right." Leaning my head against hers, "you'd be pissed if I did that to you."

Shrugging her shoulders, "whatever. Ronnie, you don't get it."

"I get it and I also heard you say that you love me."

Pulling out of my hold, "don't twist my words. What I said is that because of the way that you behave, I can't tell you that I love you."

Getting up from the bed, "same thing." Pulling my shirt over my head, "are you hungry?"

Falling back onto the bed with her feet planted on the floor, "no, and go home!"

Kneeling down between her legs, I have my chin resting on her stomach, "how long are you going to be mad at me?"

Using her left hand to push at my head, "I don't know. Maybe forever."

Grabbing her hand, I rub my thumb across the ring that I gave her, "I know you don't want to hear this, but love can make you do crazy things."

Trying to pull her hand out my grip, "control issues can make you do even crazier things."

"It feels good to know that you love me again."

Exhaling her breath, "I never said I love you." She says, in a whisper.

Raising my head to look at her, "I know what I heard."

Looking up at the ceiling, "and I know what I said." Pushing at my head so that she can sit up, "and, what I said was, you need to go home."

"Would having my baby be so bad?"

"What do you think?" She says, glaring at me. "I don't know why you keeping asking me that. I don't want nor am I trying to have a baby. Especially, not now." Moving to get up, "and you don't either."

Pulling her back down onto the bed, "so what if you're pregnant?"

Folding her arms across her chest, "what if I am. You already..."

Eyes focused on hers, "don't even say it. Better yet, don't think it. You can forget that happening. I mean it. Hell no!" Getting up from the floor, "if you ever..."

Getting up from the bed, "if I ever what? Don't threaten me!" Walking out of her bedroom, I'm right behind her ass. "My body is one thing that you definitely don't have control over."

"You know what? You're right, I need to go home before I have to hurt your smart ass!"

Hands on her hips, "really Ronnie. And I'm supposed to be scared."

Laughing out loud at her crazy ass, "I'll see you tonight."

"I don't know what's so funny and no, you will not be seeing me tonight."

Talking as if what she's saying doesn't matter, "and don't let me find out that you met up with Malcolm either. Engaged or not, I don't care. If he's engaged, then he needs to be spending time with her and leave you alone. I don't know how many times I have to remind you that you're mine. I don't share. Don't make me have to kick his ass."

Now she's pissed and it's funny as hell. "Now I know you've lost your damn mind. You can't tell me who I can and can't meet up with."

Tying my shoes, "keep talking. Just keep talking. I know how to handle your ass." Staring at me with her mouth open, I get up from the sofa, kiss her on the lips and head out the door. Damn, I love this girl! "Like I said, I'll see you tonight."

Chapter Thirty Nine
2 months later...

I finally turned in my notice at Brockman and Goldstein and to my surprise, they've asked me to stay on as a contractor. With the money they offered, minus the benefits, I couldn't refuse.

Todd wasn't too happy about my decision, but I have to do what's best for me. Besides, I don't feel that doing contract work is going to affect our new business venture at all. However, it will surely guarantee me a steady income.

I'm meeting with the guys this evening to discuss our first contract, which I'm really excited about. Todd placed a bid on the new civic center that's being built in Los Angeles a few weeks ago. After hours and hours of working on ideas, numbers and designs, we won the bid. So our meeting tonight is also a celebration.

Arriving at the restaurant, I have the worst headache. Partly, because I've been on the phone arguing with Ronnie for most of the day. He really knows how to work my nerves. If it's not one thing with him, it's another. Makes me almost regret that I ever started seeing him again. Not to mention, I still haven't gotten my period this month and the one last month wasn't really much of a cycle, it only lasted one day.

Getting out of my car, Daniel has also just arrived.

"Hey Michelle, we're late. Get ready for Todd's lecture."

"I know. I got held up at the office talking to Mr. Brockman."

"He still trying to talk you into staying on permanently?"

Smiling at him, "how'd you know?"

"Everybody knows."

Walking inside the restaurant, Todd and Felton are at the bar waiting for us. "You're late," Todd says. "Our table is ready, we're just waiting on Jason. He's in the men's room."

"Sorry man. We got held up at the office." Daniel says, looking at me with a smirk on his face.

After about two hours of going over the details of the new contract and eating dinner, I'm finally going home.

I promised Ronnie that I'd call him once the meeting was over, but I think I'm going to wait. I really need to relax first. Maybe, my period is late because of all the stress that I've been under lately with work, Ronnie, and now my mother, who according to my brother, is ill.

I haven't talked to my mother or my brothers in over six months. And to be honest, I could have gone another six months or more and it wouldn't matter to me in the least.

It's not like they call me unless they need something. Thus, the reason for Duane's call on last night.

"Hey Michelle."

"Hey."

"Have you talked to Marcus?"

"No."

"Well, the reason I'm calling is because mama is sick and needs money for her medical bills."

I'm just holding the phone because I already knew that his call involved me sending them money."

"Are you there?"

"Yes, I'm here."

"So, can you send the money or not?"

Really? Laughing to myself, *"not. I'm not sending her, you, Marcus or anybody else any money."*

"Why not?"

"Is it always about money with you guys? You never call me unless you need something. What makes you think that I have money to always shell out to you?"

"Look, I didn't want to call you but she needs help."

"Then you help her!"

"If I had it, I would."

If he had it, he would. If he had it, he wouldn't have even called. Biting the inside of my lip, I'm not helping them. I'm not. *"Duane, you need to find another way, I'm not sending her any money."*

Before he can respond, I hang up the phone.

Arriving home, I have unwanted tears flowing down my cheeks. All I've ever wanted was for my mother to love me. In all my twenty eight years, the most that I can say for our relationship is that she's been polite. Going into my bedroom, I'm going to take a hot bath to help relax the tension in my shoulders.

After my long soak in the tub, I've come to the conclusion that the stress from work is for the most part, temporary. Dealing with my family is a no-brainer, I don't have to. Exhaling a deep breath, but if I'm pregnant. Falling face down onto the bed, that's going to be a major problem. Turning onto my back, a baby means Ronnie and Ronnie means a big ass headache!

Ugh, my life!

Chapter Forty

I purchased tickets to a basketball game tonight and instead of asking Sean or Chad to go, I asked Michelle.

The game is in Los Angeles, so I suggested that we reserve a hotel there instead of driving back to San Diego. I didn't think she was going to agree but to my surprise, she did.

Hearing the doorbell, this is one of the things that pisses me off about her because she has a key that she refuses to use.

Opening the door, "why didn't you use your key?"

Closing the door behind herself, "not my house."

Looking over my shoulder, this woman! "If I had a key to your place, rest assured, I'd use it."

Going into the family room to sit, "that's why you don't have one."

"Yet."

"Never."

Smirking at her, "we'll see." Not waiting for her to respond, "I'll grab my bag so we can head out."

The drive to Los Angeles was pleasant. The game was great. Now that we're in the hotel room, she's quiet as a church house mouse. Biting the inside of her lip, she's being too damn quiet.

"Want to order a movie?"

"Yeah, sure."

"Hungry?"

"Not really. Are you hungry?"

"Nah, just trying to make conversation with you." Watching her as she flops down on the bed wearing short cotton shorts and a tank, "are you okay?"

"Yes Ronnie, I'm fine." With her elbow propped up, she's resting her head in her hand, "are you okay?"

Crawling into bed, I push her onto her back and climb on top of her, "what are you thinking about? And don't lie." Taking my fingers to pull at her lip, "you're biting the inside of you lip."

Looking up at me, "I have a lot on my mind."

Kissing her on her nose, "besides the fact that you're period is late, what else is bothering you?"

Watching the display of emotions in her eyes is a tale tell sign that I've gotten part of my assumption right. "How do you know my period is late?"

"Because I know your body. You always get your period the first of the month."

"I'm hoping it's late because of stress."

Laughing at her. "Hope on." Lowering my head to kiss her in the crook of her neck, "don't be disappointed when you find out that stress has nothing to do with it being late." I whisper in her ear.

Exhaling her breath, "that's what I'm afraid of."

Getting up from the bed, I grab my shirt. Pulling the shirt over my head, she sits up in bed. Grabbing my tennis shoes, "I'll be right back."

"Where are you going?"

"To buy a pregnancy test."

Getting up from the bed, "can't you wait until we get back to San Diego?"

"I could. But, I want to know now."

Sitting back on the bed, she has her head down. I should probably wait to find out, but if I go along with Michelle, she'll only procrastinate by waiting on a period that we both know isn't going to come.

"I'll be back."

Returning from the store, I bought two tests. One says that you can find out if you're pregnant after the first day your cycle is late. The other was recommended by the pharmacist. Throwing my keys and wallet on the table, "ready to find out?"

"Not really." Taking the tests out of the bag, she picks up the one that I chose. Reading the instructions, she gets up and goes into the bathroom. Turning to face me, she places her hand on my chest. "Can't you wait out here?"

"Oh sorry, just anxious."

Opening the door, she has the wand on the counter. Standing behind her, I have my chin resting on her shoulder. One blue line appears, she doesn't say anything. Two blue lines, she walks slowly out of the bathroom. Following her into the room, she falls face down on the bed. "Oh God!" She says, resting her forehead on her folded arms.

Going to sit down on the bed next to her, I know she's upset. Rubbing the back of her leg, "what are you thinking?"

"You don't want to know."

Recalling our last conversation, "actually, I do."

"Believe me, you don't."

Lying back on the bed so that I'm right beside her, "tell me."

"Ronnie, if I tell you what I'm thinking, you're going to get upset." Sighing, "I'll just keep my thoughts to myself."

Looking up at the ceiling, "I know that you feel that this is bad timing and all because it doesn't fall in line with your plans. But babe, life happens. I'm not going to lie, I'm really happy about you being pregnant with my baby."

Turning to look at me, "how can you say that? A baby is what caused part of the problems in our marriage."

"Immaturity was the cause of our problems. Not the last pregnancy."

"It doesn't matter, I don't want this baby. I have too much going on right now. I don't want to have to be responsible for anyone other than myself, I..."

Abruptly sitting up in bed, I'm holding up my hand because I can't take anymore of her shit. "Stop! Okay. Stop acting like a spoiled ass brat. All this 'I' shit is getting on my fucking nerves."

Sitting up in bed on her knees, "getting on your nerves? Really? This time, it's your fault. I told you I wasn't on the pill and like I didn't say anything, you refused to use a condom!"

"What the hell are you talking about? I told you before, I don't feel that I should have to wear a condom with you. I said it then, I'm saying it now!" Pacing back and forth, "so we're having a baby." Flailing my hands in the air, "big deal."

"It is a big deal for me." She responds, sitting down on the bed, "but of course, like always, you're only thinking of yourself."

Sitting on the bed beside her, "I don't understand why you're overreacting. We're adults. We love each other. We're financially stable and together, we can take care of our baby."

"That's just it, we," using her finger to point between us, "are not stable. Our relationship isn't stable. We aren't committed to each other."

"Since when? We've already had this conversation." Grabbing her hand, "I love you, Michelle. I'm not going anywhere."

Covering her face with her hands, "why couldn't you have just worn a condom?" She's asking, her voice just above a whisper.

"Honestly, I didn't want to. I wanted you without a barrier. I knew each time there was a possibility that you could get pregnant, but it didn't matter to me."

Gazing at me, "so in other words, you got me pregnant on purpose."

Shrugging my shoulders, "I wouldn't say I did it on purpose, I'm just saying... hell Michelle, I don't know. I'll say this, I don't regret not wearing a condom."

"Obviously," she says getting up to go into the bathroom, closing the door behind her.

Chapter Forty One

Sitting on the toilet with my face in my hands, all I can do is cry. This is bad timing. Whether he wants to admit or not, this is bad timing.

I don't want this baby. I already have too much on my plate with my mother being sick and needing money, working under contract with Brockman and Goldstein, dealing with him and hoping all goes well with this new bid, it's too much!

Knocking on the door, "Michelle, can I come in?"

Rolling my eyes heavenward, like me saying no is going to matter. "Ronnie, can't you give me a few minutes to process my thoughts?"

"I was thinking we could do that together."

If I had a weapon, I'd seriously hurt him right now. Getting up from the toilet to open the door, I walk past him to get into bed without saying anything.

Feeling the bed dip, he's behind me with his arm thrown around my waist and his head is resting on my shoulder. "Babe, I'm sorry."

I can't wait to hear this. Rolling my eyes, "for what?"

"Not considering you and how you'd feel. I should have pulled out or worn protection like you asked."

"In other words, for getting me pregnant on purpose."

Pulling me closer, "I'll never admit to that. However, I do feel that if God didn't want us to have another baby, then you wouldn't be pregnant."

Turning my head to look at him over my shoulder, "are you seriously blaming God for this? If so, I need to get out of this bed before he strikes you dead."

Laughing, "I'm just saying that everything happens for a reason."

Taking a deep breath, "have you ever heard me ever mention anything about wanting kids? Even when I was pregnant before, did I ever mention wanting a baby while we were dating?"

Cupping my breast, "no, I don't recall you ever saying anything."

"Do you know why?" I'm asking, without giving him time to answer. "It's because I've never wanted children. Ever."

"I want babies, Michelle. I know we didn't discuss it when we were married, but I've always wanted a family."

"I don't. Even when I got pregnant before, it wasn't because I wanted the baby. I didn't want to lose you."

Frustration evident in his breathing and the fact that his hand has moved away from my breast, "what are you saying, you want an abortion?"

Frowning, "I don't believe in abortions. I'm trying to tell you how I feel."

Not saying anything for a while, he lets out a deep, heavy breath. "I hear what you're saying and believe it or not, I care about how you're feeling. Just know, this time around, you're not alone."

Feeling the need to change the subject, "I'm going to attend my Aunt Mary's fiftieth birthday celebration on next weekend."

"Really? Mind if I go with you?"

Yes, I mind. "I didn't think you'd want to attend."

"Are you kidding, I love your Aunt Mary. Besides, I can't have you and my baby on the highway alone."

Ugh! Here we go. Just found out that I'm pregnant and in Ronnie fashion, he's going to try and assert his control. "San Bernardino is only an hour and half drive."

"I know. I still want to go."

Chapter Forty Two

Michelle and I are headed to San Bernardino for her Aunt Mary's birthday party. We haven't talked much about the pregnancy. But, she has an appointment scheduled for next Tuesday with her obstetrician after receiving confirmation two days ago that we are indeed pregnant.

Arriving to the party, the family is in full force. I love this side of Michelle's family. Everyone's successful in their own right.

All the men are in different parts of the house, so I decide to go into the den, which looks more like Aiden's man cave, to catch the basketball game that's being aired on the television.

"See you in here watching the game." Michelle's dad, Mitch says, entering the room.

"Yeah, I forgot to set the recorder when I left home."

Going into the refrigerator located behind the bar, he hands me a beer as he takes a seat in one of the recliners. "I'm was glad to see you here with Michelle."

Nodding my head. I'm really trying to watch this game.

Thinking our conversation is over because of the prolonged silence, he starts talking. "You know Ronnie, it's my fault that Michelle is the way she is. Once you've hurt her, she can forgive, but she will never forget."

Glancing over at him, "I think we're doing okay."

"That's good to hear, she doesn't talk to me much." Clearing his throat, "she doesn't talk to her mother much either. Did you know that she's sick?"

Man! I just want to watch the game. Can't Mitch find someone else to talk to? "No, I didn't know."

"Yeah, she's sick. I heard that Duane called Michelle to ask for money to help with Janice's medical expenses and she told him no."

Rubbing my hand down the back of my neck, "she hasn't mentioned anything to me about Janice being sick."

"When I met Janice, I nearly lost my damned mind. She was different. A hell of a lot different than the women from my side of the tracks. She was working as a receptionist at the bank. I was working as a loan officer at the time and man, when I tell you that she was fine. She was fine." Taking a drink from his beer, "anyways, we started flirting back and forth and things started moving really fast. After about two dates, I found out that she was a single mom with two sons."

Guess I can forget about watching the game. Taking a deep breath, "wait, Marcus and Duane aren't your sons?"

"Hell nah!" Taking another drink from his beer, "he up and left them when she was pregnant with Duane." Laughing to himself, "that girl was so out there that if she had asked my ass to rob a bank, I would have." Shaking his head, "when I met her boys, I felt sorry for them. They were four and six at the time and she was struggling to make ends meet. I don't know why I did it, but after dating only three months, I asked her to marry me. Man, my folks were so pissed, they basically disowned me."

"Because she had two kids?"

"Because she had two kids. Because we were from different economic backgrounds. Because she had never been married to her boy's daddy and the list goes on."

"Damn."

"Yeah, damn." Rubbing his hand down his face, "she was twenty one and I was twenty three. I was so whipped, I didn't even consider the responsibility that went along with raising two boys who weren't mine, but I tried. Yeah, I tried." He sighs. "After about six months into our marriage, I wanted out. I didn't want to bail on her like her ex did so I told her that maybe if we had a baby, things would get better." Sniffling out loud, "wrong. She told me from the beginning that she didn't want more kids and I should have listened. She finally gave in and got pregnant. Instead of things getting better, they got worse. She was spending my money left and right. Had us in so much debt, I couldn't think straight. And her boys, those bastards were bad as hell."

"That's not hard to believe."

Getting up to get another beer, "she would get mad as hell when I tried to discipline them. Telling me that I wasn't their daddy and there I was, the one taking care of them. After a while, I just gave up."

Closing his eyes, "the night Michelle was born, I was so happy. I remember her words so clear, 'I didn't want no girl, she going to be too much trouble.' Here I was, a first time dad and all she could say was, she didn't want the baby that she carried in her body for nine months. At that point, I decided I wasn't going to put myself or my daughter through that so Michelle literally went from the hospital to my mother's. I was the one who named her because Janice refused to."

Rubbing my hand down my face, maybe it's not such a coincidence that Mitch came in here after all. "Wow, that's crazy."

Taking a drink from his beer, "I thought she was going to come around and demand that I bring Michelle back to her, but she never did. And anytime that Michelle would go there to visit, she was mistreated. Long story short, my parent's raised Michelle. When my dad died, my mother and Michelle were thick as thieves. She didn't want for anything." Laughing out loud, "they had her involved in everything. All I did was write the checks."

Taking a deep breath, "when Michelle was fifteen, my mother got sick. When the doctor's gave up and said there was nothing else they could do, she asked me to please watch over her princess and not to send her to live with her mother. I didn't know that she had already asked my sisters to take Michelle in. Carolyn was living overseas with her husband and their three boys and Mary was living over in Fairfield with her husband and four boys and barely getting by so, I was my mother's last resort to take care of my daughter."

Michelle never told me any of this. Now the game that I was watching prior to Mitch coming in here is no longer interesting. Neither is the beer that he gave me, I haven't even touched it.

"The day my mother died, Michelle was so sad. She stayed to herself the entire time. We had a house full of people who were basically catering to her because they all knew how close she was to her grandmother, but she just stayed to herself." Hearing him get choked up with emotion, "about a month later, I came in and told Michelle that I couldn't take care of her. I told her that she had to go to her mother's temporarily." Shaking his head, "all because I met a woman who didn't want to be bothered with my child."

"Wait, Michelle was a teenager."

"Michelle was a spoiled teenager who demanded time and attention. Like I said, she was involved in everything." Taking a deep breath, "she begged me not to take her there. Told me that she'd drop out of all activities, just please, don't take me to her. I was too selfish to think about what she wanted, so I called her mother." Wiping at his tears that have been streaming down his face for a while now, "I was able to convince Janice to take her in by promising to pay her a thousand dollars a month. It was always something going on over there and Janice was always asking for more money. Why, I still don't know because the only activities that Michelle was involved in was through the school, and they were free." Clearing his throat, "my baby girl graduated with honors and was able to attend college on a full academic scholarship. I would send her checks while she was in school and she never cashed not one of them. I still don't know how she survived because it wasn't with my help."

I should get up and beat the shit out of him for what he did but I don't have to, he's already beaten down. "She worked her butt off. She stayed focused and she didn't allow anything to get in her way." Now it's clear.

"She talks to Linda from time to time. That's how I'm able to find out what's going on with her. She doesn't talk to me at all and when she does, her words are few."

"Mitch, have you apologized to her?"

Looking at me, "many, many, many times and she says she's forgiven me, but I honestly can't tell." Crying into his hands, "I let her down. When she needed me most, I let her down. I knew she was being mistreated. I just didn't want to be responsible for her at the time." Leaning over in the recliner, he's pulling out his handkerchief from his back pocket, "Ronnie, I've made it hard for you. Michelle loves you. I know she does. You hurt her. Hurt her so much that she'll never give you the opportunity to do it again. She's got a strong will." Blowing his nose, "my mother left her a trust that she was privy to when she turned twenty five. It wasn't until my sister provided proof that the money was from her grandmother and not me, that she accepted it."

"Wow." Michelle mentioned that she used some of the money that her grandmother had left for her to invest in her business venture, but she didn't elaborate too much, and I didn't ask. Her money has always been hers.

"I want so much to have a relationship with her."

Thinking about how far Michelle and I have come, I know she has a loving and forgiving heart. "Mitch, maybe you should try to talk to her again. Maybe there's something you haven't said to her in your conversations before that might help. I don't know. I see your hurt and maybe that's what she needs to see. I can't tell you."

Getting up from his recliner, "thanks for listening Ronnie."

"Anytime."

Chapter Forty Three

Giving my Aunt Mary a hug while waiting for Ronnie, she leans in so that only I hear what she has to say, "remember baby, no one is perfect. That man loves you. Everyone can see it. Don't let the fear of your past keep you from being happy." Cupping the side of my face, "you deserve to be happy Michelle."

Trying to hold back the tears that are threatening to fall, "thank you Aunt Mary, I'll keep that in mind." Hugging her again, "I'm so glad I came, I've missed you so much."

Ronnie is in the family room talking to my Aunt Carolyn, when Mitch approaches me, "did you enjoy yourself today?"

Avoiding eye contact with him, "I had a good time." Still staring at Ronnie, he looks up at me and smiles.

"Michelle, I want you to know that I love you."

Still staring at Ronnie, "okay."

Touching my shoulder, I flinch. "Can you look at me? Please?"

I'm keeping my focus on Ronnie, "what do you want, Mitch?"

Hearing the emotion in his voice, he hesitates before speaking, "I want my daughter to forgive me for not being there for her. I want her to know that I'm so sorry for making her go through hell because I was too selfish to do what was right." Turning to look at him, "I want her to know that I regret ever hurting her and putting my needs before her own. I want her to know that I'm so proud of her and all of her accomplishments."

Tears streaming down my face, I can't stop crying. Reaching out to grab his hand, he's crying too. In a whisper, "I forgive you, daddy." Grabbing me into a tight hug, I hear him sobbing, saying over and over again how sorry he is. I'm not sure how long we've been standing like this or who is watching, but at this moment, I don't care. My dad's betrayal hurt me more than anything. I was hurt behind my grandmother's death too, but I didn't want to see her suffer. However, sending me to live with a woman, who on a daily basis reminded me that I wasn't wanted, was unforgivable. And now, with him truly acknowledging what he did wrong…Aunt Mary is right, no one is perfect. How can I expect God to forgive me for my many wrongdoings if I'm not willing to forgive those who've hurt me? Letting go of this pain, I feel so free.

"I'm sorry baby girl, I'm not holding you too tight am I?"

Laughing, "I'm okay. Thank you."

"No sweetheart, thank you. Giving me another hug, "oh and Michelle, try not to be so hard on Ronnie. That man loves you."

"I know."

Walking in our direction, Ronnie has that look of concern written all over his face. "You okay?"

Smiling through my tears, "I'm okay."

Chapter Forty Four

I'm thirty four weeks along in my pregnancy, which, for the most part, has gone by rather smoothly with the exception of Ronnie.

Lately, all we do is argue. We've argued about everything from me not wanting to marry him before the baby is born, to me spending too much time working with the guys, to why did you have to meet Malcolm for lunch? Everything with him is an argument.

Like now, we're at his house, in his bedroom, arguing back and forth over names for the baby. "I like the name Morgan. It's a strong name, with class. I want my daughter to be strong and confident."

Staring at him, "all I asked was if we could put 'Elizabeth' in there somewhere." Getting up from the bed, I'm stepping into my flats.

"Morgan Elizabeth Wen. I like that name." Scowling at me, "why are you putting on your shoes?"

Exhaling my breath, "I'm going home."

"Why? You just got here. I thought you were staying the night."

"I changed my mind." Looking at him, "I'm tired of arguing with you about every little thing. You're stressing me out with this constant bickering about nothing."

"You hanging out with Malcolm all damn day is not a *little thing*," he says with emphasis. Getting up from the bed, "I'm going with you. If he's really engaged, let him eat lunch with her ass. I'm sure she was probably hungry too."

Looking at him, "you really need help, Ronnie. Do you ever listen to the crap that comes out of your mouth? And no, I don't want you going home with me." He just wants sex. Hell, I want it too. I think it's the only time we're not arguing.

Grabbing me from behind, he leans down to kiss the back of my neck, "babe, please, don't go."

Turning around, I look up into his eyes, "you just want to have sex," raising my hand, "excuse me, to make love."

Smiling down at me, "hell yeah, that's what I want. Soon, we won't be able to."

Snidely smiling at him, "strip down and get on the bed."

"Ah shit! I hope like hell this Michelle sticks around after Morgan gets here."

Removing my sweater and jeans, "just remember, this Michelle, is driven by hormones."

Lying back on the bed, looking good as hell, he has his hands up to help me position myself as I straddle him. "Guess I'm going to have to keep this Michelle pregnant then."

Smiling down at him, I'm shaking my head, "that's not going to happen." Easing down onto his very erect penis, I begin to slowly move up and down. "Am I too heavy?"

Opening his eyes, he shakes his head, "no babe. I'm trying not to cum." He says, through clenched teeth. "You're perfect." Placing his hands on my hips, he starts thrusting into me in bold, steady strokes.

Throwing my head back, I cum. Hard. "Ah, um!"

Squeezing my hips, I watch him as he releases. Opening his eyes, he stares back at me. "Baby, I love you so much. You know that, right?"

Nodding my head, I still haven't uttered the words that have been on the tip of my tongue since we first heard our baby's heartbeat.

"I know you do. You don't have to say it now. Eventually, you will."

Helping me as I move off of him, "I am so huge. I hope I get my body back when this is over."

"I think you look beautiful." Touching my stomach, the baby kicks. Smiling up at me, he leans forward replacing his hand with his lips, "daddy loves you too, princess."

Each time he does this, I get a bit emotional. I love this baby so much. It took some time for me to realize it, but now that I know this love, I don't have as many regrets.

Helping me to get up from the bed, "have you talked to your mother?"

Slowly turning to look at him, "why?"

Clearing his throat, "Marcus called and said that she's not doing well." Watching my expression, he holds up his hand. "Babe, he called me because he said that he left you several messages."

Ever since Ronnie talked to my dad, he acts like he has some kind of insight into my life. I don't like it because it forces me to have to address certain issues that are dead to me. Sad to say, Janice is dead to me. The only reason that they've been calling me is for money. According to a message from Marcus, she's on dialysis. "No, I haven't and if you want me to stay, drop it."

Going into the bathroom ahead of me, he turns on the shower. "I'm going to drop it for now. Sooner or later, you need to talk to her." Looking back at me, "hard to forgive someone when they're dead."

Glaring at him, "they're only calling me for money! She doesn't and has never given a damn about me, so why should I waste my time calling her when I know I'm not going to help."

"Calm down. Why are you yelling?"

"I'm not yelling. I already told you that I don't want to talk about this crap."

"You are yelling." Dropping his head, "you haven't even told them about our baby."

Rolling my eyes, why won't he let this go? "It's not like they're ever going to see her."

Stepping into the shower, he holds his hand out to help me inside. Exhaling his breath, he looks disappointed in me. "Handle it your way then. I was just relaying the message."

Lying in bed, Ronnie's asleep and I'm wide awake. My emotions are all over the place concerning Janice. This woman, my mother, has never once told me that she even liked me. Closing my eyes, all I can do is pray and ask God for guidance.

Getting out of bed, it's after eleven, but it's now or never. Grabbing my cell phone, I go into the den to make my dreaded call. After the third ring, she answers.

"Hello." She says in a groggy voice.

"Hi Janice, this is Michelle."

"I know who this is." Coughing, "so you finally decided to call me, huh?"

"Duane and Marcus called and said that you're sick."

"They called you months ago."

"I know."

"I hear you're having a baby."

"Yeah."

"Heard Ronnie's excited about his little girl."

"Yeah, he is."

"When y'all getting married again."

Wiping at a tear that has managed to escape, "not sure if I'm going to get remarried."

"Why not? You having his baby. He love you. Might as well."

"It's not that simple."

"Girl, taking care of babies is hard work. You gone need his help."

I can't believe she of all people is saying this to me. "We don't have to be married for him to help."

"Y'all living together?"

Frowning, "no, I have my own place."

"So this little girl is gone have to go between houses."

Okay, I've had enough of this. "Look, I just called to check on you."

"I'm fine, Michelle."

"Well, I'll let you go. I realize it's late."

"Michelle, listen. Please don't hang up. I know I hurt you. You never have to call me again. I just want you to know that in my own way, I love you. I loved you then. I was a very bitter, angry, broken woman at the time and I didn't know how to show you."

Did she just say that she loves me? Feeling the tears streaming down my face, I'm covering my mouth to keep from crying out.

"When I met your father, I was at a low place in my life. And here he comes in to save the world. Only problem was, he couldn't save me. I had never healed from being abused by my own father, by the boy's daddy and in some ways, by your father."

Going silent, "are you there?"

"Yes, I'm here." I say, in a whisper.

"When you were born, all I could think was, how can I protect this baby girl? Who protected me? Then I had to watch you be loved by Mitch's parents." Coughing, "I was so damn envious of you. So envious that in some ways, I thought that I hated you." Sounding like she too is crying, "when you came to live with me, I tried to break you. The harder I tried, the harder you worked to get away. Just like everybody else, you wanted to get away."

Finding my voice, "you were always so mean to me. For no reason at all, you were mean. Which is why I didn't want this baby in the beginning. I honestly feared what type of mother I might be. But the longer I carry her, the more I love her. How could you not love a child that you carried inside of your body?"

"When you don't love yourself, it's easy."

"You loved Duane and Marcus. You always have."

"They was boys. You're a girl. What you are, what you possess, I could have never instilled those values in you."

"Did you ever try?" Now, I'm audibly crying. "There were times when I really needed you, Janice. Even though my grandparents loved me, I wanted your love. When kids talked about their mother's, there were times when I would pray that you would spend time with me. Just you and me, without all the yelling and hitting."

"I didn't know how to try."

"I remember the time Marcus punched me in the face for correcting something that he said, you could have protected me then, but you didn't. You sat there and laughed."

"Michelle, I'm not proud of that."

"And when I got married. I didn't want to marry Ronnie. I really needed you then. You weren't there. You have no idea how badly I needed you."

"You were pregnant. You did the right thing."

"No, I didn't. Do you have any idea how unhappy I was in my marriage? On top of being unhappy, you didn't make it any easier by always calling and asking for money."

"We needed help. Family is supposed to help each other."

"No. That's not true. We're supposed to help ourselves. You used us like an ATM."

Humming into the phone, "is that why you didn't send the money when Duane called?"

"I'm not your ATM. I'm not giving you anything else. I don't owe you anything, Janice. It seems my whole life, I've been repaying you for being born."

"Is that how you feel?"

"Yes, that's exactly how I feel."

"Then I'm sorry. I'm really sorry and I hope you can find it in your heart to forgive me. You turned out fine. You a fine young woman and I'm so proud of you." Coughing, "if I don't talk to you again, you take care of that baby."

Wiping my tears, I feel so clean. Completely free. It's like a ton of bricks have rolled off my shoulders. "Take care of yourself and Janice, I forgive you and I hope that you can forgive me too. Thank you for talking to me."

"It doesn't have to be our last conversation. I know I messed up with you, but I'd love to make up for it with my grand-daughter. Do you have a name for her yet?"

I'm not sure about taking my baby around her. I'll have to really think long and hard about that. "Her name is Morgan. She's due on February fifth."

"February fifth, I've got to mark my calendar. So young lady, are you going to remarry that young man for this baby's sake?"

Exhaling my breath and still trying to calm by breathing from crying, "I don't know. Like I said before, it's not that simple."

"Pray about it. God will work it all out." Laughing, "He works in mysterious ways. Who would have thought that He'd answer my prayer at eleven at night?"

"You prayed about me calling you?"

"For over a year now. And look, you called."

Smiling, "thank you, Janice. I'll keep what you said in mind."

"Love you. Don't let this be our last conversation."

"Okay. Bye."

Leaning back against the sofa, I'm crying. This time, they aren't sad tears. These are happy tears. The heavy weight is gone. "Thank you, Lord."

Chapter Forty Five

Michelle and I are headed to Bakersfield today for her baby shower. I tried to talk my sisters into coming to San Diego, but they insisted on us coming to Bakersfield.

Reaching over to place my hand on top of her stomach, "comfortable?"

Looking up from her phone, "no." Exhaling her breath, "I'm miserable."

"Two more weeks. You only have two more weeks."

Biting the inside of her lip, she closes her eyes. "Two more weeks. Maybe, she'll come early."

"Yeah, maybe." Focusing on the road, I've been dancing around talking to her again about us all living under one roof. She's made it perfectly clear that she's unsure about marriage. The last time I mentioned us living together, she went off. Pinching the bridge of my nose, "Um Michelle, have you thought about what would happen if you were to go into labor while you're home alone?"

Typing something into her phone, which is pissing me off, she looks out the window. Exhaling her breath, "I have." Looking at her phone, she frowns. Rubbing at her temple, "I'd call you or I'd drive myself."

Eyebrows raised, "that's your plan." Laughing to myself, "you better come up with another one. I have two sisters who've both had babies," looking at her out the corner of my eye, "it may not go down like you're planning."

Obviously, she's stressed about something, "I don't know, Ronnie. I'll give it some more thought."

"What's wrong? Who are you texting?"

"Todd and Jason." Looking at her phone, "the numbers are off for the complex. I told them that over a week ago." Laying her head against the seat. "I think Jason is trying to blame it on me."

"Why would he do something like that?"

"I don't know. Maybe he's not, but it seems like it." Answering her phone, *"hey, Felton. Yeah, I know. I'm feeling the same way. I know. Well, I just forwarded another copy of my report to Todd which has mention of the numbers being off. He said that?"* Looking out the window, she looks like she's about to cry. *"I'm pulling my weight, Felton. Whatever. You know what, I'm going to call Todd and tell him to kiss my ass. This is not my fault. Okay. You too. Bye."*

"What did he say?"

"Apparently, Todd didn't review my report and went with the report that Jason gave him." Answering her phone, *"hello. Yeah, whatever. You know what Todd, kiss my ass. I'm tired of you trying to trickle every mishap to being my mistake. My numbers are always accurate and you know it. Don't blame me that you didn't do your part. Well, you're right. I am and you know what, I have bigger problems to deal with than being bothered by your bullshit!"* Hanging up the phone, she's crying.

Grabbing her hand, I don't want to say anything that will upset her any more than she already is, so I'll wait on my suggestion of us living together.

Arriving to Sharon's house, I put the car in park and turn in my seat to face her. "Listen babe, I know you're upset by what happened with Todd. But, this is your day. Try not to think about work. Just relax and have fun. And remember, you don't have to work. You're only working because you want to."

Smiling at me, she leans forward and kisses me on the lips. "Thank you, Ronnie."

What? Normally, she'd be going off about taking care of herself. Maybe I should ask her now? Nah, I'll wait. Getting out of the car, I go around to open the door for her.

Before we can ring the doorbell, Michael Jr., opens the door and jumps into my arms, "Uncle Ronnie, I haven't seen you in forever."

Hugging him, "you just saw me at Christmas."

"That was a long time ago." He says, giggling, "Hi Auntie Michelle."

Smiling at him, "hi MJ." She says, going into the house.

Coming around the corner, Rhonda pulls Michelle into a hug, "hey girl, you look like you're about to pop."

Placing her left hand on top of her stomach, "I feel like I'm about to pop."

"I remember those days and I don't miss them at all!" Turning back to look at me, "hey, Ronnie."

"Rhonda."

"The men are in Aiden's man cave." She says, giving me a sly smile. Michelle has no idea that her aunts, step-mom and Yolanda are all here to celebrate with her.

Taking MJ's hand, I hear her scream, "oh my God! I can't believe you all are here."

Tugging on my hand, "Uncle Ronnie, girls are silly."

Laughing at him, "don't let your mother hear you say that."

"My mommy is silly too." He says, through his giggles.

"What's so funny?" Sean is asking, as we enter the cave.

"Your nephew here thinks that girls are silly."

Walking over to take a seat on the sofa, Aiden, Sebastian and Sean are playing cards, while Michael, Rhonda's husband, is sitting on the sofa watching television. "What's up fellas?"

"What's up with you, man?" Aiden is asking.

"Not much. Ready for this pregnancy to be over with."

"Michelle driving you crazy?" Sebastian is asking.

"Crazy is not even the word for what goes on with her. It's like she has two personalities."

Rubbing the top of MJ's head. "I remember when Rhonda was pregnant with our boys. Man, the last few weeks were insane. She was either complaining or crying. I never knew what to expect when I came home." Nodding his head with his brows raised, "I don't envy you at all."

Rolling his eyes, "and yet, you knocked her up three times." Sean says. "You fools are stupid. You know what I don't get, Ronnie?"

Glaring at him, "what don't you get, Sean?"

Looking at the cards in his hand, he glances up, "now, this is what I heard, so I'm only asking...did you knock Michelle up on purpose to stop her from dating some dude?"

Glancing over at Aiden. "Man, who told you that?"

"Why the hell you looking at me? I haven't said anything to anybody."

"Hey fellas, my son is sitting here."

Staring over at Michael, everyone says at the same time, "and!" Leaning back in his chair, "his ass should be outside playing with the other kids anyway." Sean says.

"Sean, man, who told you that?"

"So, it's true?"

Cracking up laughing, Sebastian looks at me. "Ronnie, it's okay. You did what you had to do to get your woman back."

"Man, shut the fuck up! Sean, who told you that shit?"

Smiling, "is it true or not?"

"Ronnie, calm down. Nobody told Sean that. He's just messing with you." Aiden says, getting up from the table. "I'm going to grab some more beers." Holding out his hand, "come on MJ. Let's go find you some boys your age to play with."

Getting up from the sofa, I need to talk to this fool. Sitting down in the chair that Aiden just vacated, "man seriously, who told you that?"

"Actually, I overhead mom talking to Rhonda and Mrs. Linda about it."

"When?"

"Earlier today." Looking up at Sebastian, he slowly brings his attention back to me, "don't say anything."

"I won't."

"I'm serious. You can't say anything."

"I said I won't say nothing. Now tell me."

"I heard mom say that she's glad Michelle finally came around to accepting her pregnancy because she heard that you're the one who wanted to this baby and not Michelle."

Why would she say something like that? As if reading my mind. "I think it has to do with something that Rhonda overheard Yolanda say because I heard her name mentioned a few times."

"I can't stand that girl!"

"So, did you?"

I should go out there and cuss that skank out. I can't stand her ass. "Nah, I didn't purposely get her pregnant, I just didn't bother using protection."

Sebastian, Sean and Michael all look at each other before looking at me, "man, you did that shit on purpose."

"Y'all shut the hell up. I didn't do nothing. Sean, is that all that was said?"

Covering his mouth while laughing out loud, "that's all I heard, but I'd bet money that there's more to this story."

Getting up from the table, "Sean, grow the hell up!"

I'm really enjoying this baby shower. After the morning that I've had, this is just what I needed. Being able to see my aunts and Yolanda really means a lot to me. I've got to make sure to thank Rhonda and Sharon for including them.

"Okay, now that we've all eaten, let's open the gifts." Sharon says. "Michelle, you sit over here in the mommy chair."

As I'm moving to sit in the chair that Sharon has in the middle of the room, I notice Ronnie walking towards me with a pissed off look on his face. "What's wrong? You look upset."

"I'm fine." He says, squatting down next to me, "enjoying your shower?"

Smiling at him, "yes. I'm having a good time."

"That's good. Thought I'd come check on you."

Before I can respond, "Ronnie, you ready for this baby?"

"Yes, Aunt Lucy. We're ready."

"Your father tells me that you aren't planning to get remarried. If that's true, then how are you ready? In Asian custom, a man should be married to the mother of his child."

Looking at Ronnie out the corner of my eye, he is pissed about something. "We're ready." He says, in a clipped tone. "And, I don't think its Asian custom, it's your opinion."

"Listen Aunt Lucy," Rhonda says with her hands up, "let's not get into this right now. Ronnie and Michelle are adults. Whatever and however they decide to handle their business, is their business."

"That's foolishness." My Aunt Carolyn says. "Business my ass! I don't understand you young people. You sit around playing house and the baby is the one who suffers." Looking at me, "Michelle you know better. If you forgave this man enough to continue to spread your legs for him, then you should be able to get married before this baby is born."

"Carolyn, this is none of your business."

"Shut the hell up, Mary. That's Michelle's problem, she's spoiled and nobody ever tells her when she's wrong. And Ronnie, son, you should be worried. Am I the only one who noticed that this girl hasn't shown the least bit of interest in these kids running around here all day? A soon to be mom usually shows some sign of motherly instinct. But not this one." She says, pointing at me. "You know…"

"Ladies, ladies. That's enough." Ronnie's mom interjects. "This is not the time, nor the place for…"

"No! We need to get to the bottom of this." Aunt Lucy is now saying.

What is going on? Glancing around the room, everyone is either in shock or waiting for more action to pop off. Getting ready to check my Aunt Carolyn. I know damn well she's not trying to imply…

"First of all, we don't owe y'all shit! Ronnie says, standing to his feet. "What the hell you mean we need to get to the bottom of this?"

"Now, Ronnie."

Holding up his hand, "no mom. Enough is enough. This is a fucking shower and y'all in here trying to put your two cents in on something that doesn't concern you." Looking over at my Aunt Carolyn, "and no. I'm not worried. Our baby is going to be fine." Grabbing my hand, "come on, Michelle. Let's go."

"Ronnie, wait. You can't leave yet. We haven't even opened the gifts." Sharon says.

"We're leaving, we don't need this shit!"

Squeezing his hand, "Ronnie, wait." Looking at Sharon, "we'll be back." Stepping outside, into their backyard, "what are you upset about?"

Pointing towards the house, "them. We don't need this shit."

"You were upset when you came into the room. What happened?"

Looking out into the yard, "did you tell Yolanda that I got you pregnant on purpose?"

"What?"

Scowling at me, "you heard me. Did you tell her that shit?"

"I never said that you did it on purpose, but I did say that you refused to wear condoms."

"Why did you tell her that?"

Frowning at him, "why not? She's my friend. We tell each other stuff."

"Well, your *friend* was blabbing her mouth because Sean said that he overhead my mom and Rhonda talking about it."

"That's crazy."

Glaring at me, "crazy. Crazy huh? What's crazy is the fact that my brother thinks I got you pregnant so that you wouldn't end up with that fuck, Malcolm."

"Did he really say that?" Placing my hand on the lower part of my stomach, I wince.

Rubbing his hand down the back of his head, "are you in pain or is the baby kicking?"

Letting out a deep breath, "she's kicking." Placing my other hand on top of my stomach, "I don't care what they say or think in there, this is my life. I have to do what I feel is best for me." Looking into his eyes, "I also know what Aunt Carolyn was trying to imply and just so you know, I love my baby."

"I know you love our baby." He says, in a whisper.

Looking up at him, I turn so that we're facing each other. "I love you too."

"I already knew that." He says, leaning down to kiss me.

Kissing him back, "um hmm. So I guess I didn't have to tell you then, huh."

Wrapping his arms around my extremely wide waist, "I'm glad you told me."

"Babe, don't let what they're talking about bother you so much that it takes you out of character. They're entitled to have an opinion. It doesn't mean we have go along with them. Your sisters went through a lot to put this shower together. It wouldn't be fair to them to leave."

Touching his forehead to mine, "maybe I'm upset because there's some truth to what they're saying in there. Our baby needs to be in a stable environment, Michelle. We can't give her that living in different households."

Looking back towards the house, I turn to glance up at him, "what if things don't work out with us living under the same roof?"

"Babe, we have to trust each other and make it work. Our baby deserves a healthy home."

Biting the inside of my lip, I don't want to talk about this right now. I have too much other stuff going on. Closing my eyes, I let out a deep breath.

Pulling at my bottom lip, "I don't want to pressure you and like I've said before, I love you. I will never do anything to intentionally hurt you again. I promise." Tilting my head back, he kisses me, "do you trust me?" Nodding my head. Smiling, "I trust you too."

Frowning up at him, "I've never given you any reason not to trust me."

Eyebrows raised, "yeah, you have."

After a few minutes of going back and forth with each other, "we better go back in there before the *two aunts* decide to come out here and go postal on us."

"I know, right." Holding my hand as we're walking back towards the house, "I've never liked my Aunt Carolyn. I'm kinda glad you told her old butt off."

"They were both overdue for a good cuss out." He says, making us both laugh.

Finally, the shower has come to an end. Thank God for my Aunt Mary, Rhonda, Sharon, Camille and Yolanda. In spite of all the tension in the room when we came back inside from our talk, they were able to pull everyone together and we ended up having a lot of fun.

"Friend, it looks like you're going home in one piece. "Yolanda says, coming to stand next to me. "Those aunts are fierce."

"No thanks to you, big mouth."

"I'm sorry! I said it in a joking manner." When I came back inside, I asked her about what Ronnie said and sure enough, she told Camille. "Are you up for company later tonight?"

"Don't you have an early flight?"

"I do." She says, moving her eyebrows up and down, "It leaves out of San Diego. I know you didn't think we came all this way for me not to hang out with my girl." She says, wrapping her arm around my shoulders.

"Girl, why didn't you tell me? If I had known you were staying in San Diego, I would have bailed a long time ago. Hold up...did you say we?"

"Um hmm. Sure did."

Feeling Ronnie's hand on my back, "babe, you ready?" He's asking, completely ignoring Yolanda.

Laughing through my nose, Ronnie can be so immature at times. "Alright Yolanda, call me when you get to San Diego."

"I will." She says, rolling her eyes at Ronnie. "Oh, is it okay for Daren to come along?"

"Of course. Where is he now?"

"On his way to pick me up." She says, hugging me. "We'll see you later." Glaring at Ronnie, "bye, Ronnie."

"Bye, skank." He says under his breath.

Turning to look at him, "that was so rude." Shaking my head as I'm walking away, "I can't believe you just called her that."

"I can't stand her ass."

"Really? Who would have ever guessed?"

"Where are you going?"

"To thank your mom and sisters."

Chapter Forty Six

We're on our way back home and of course, Michelle is mad at me for what I said about her stank friend.

Glancing over at her, "what do you want to do tonight?" Acting as if I didn't hear her talking to *her friend.*

"Yolanda and Daren are coming over."

"What about us? I thought we were going to hang out together."

"I don't recall you saying anything about us hanging out together tonight." Placing her hand on the left side of her stomach, she blows out a deep breath.

Frowning over at her, I put my hand on top of her stomach, "I just assumed we would."

Looking at me out the corner of her eye, "well, you know what they say about assumptions."

"No, I don't know anything about that. Anyways, why wouldn't we be together tonight?" Rubbing my hand down my face, "see, this is the shit I'm talking about. If we were living *under the same roof*, this wouldn't even be an issue."

Moving around in her seat, "if we were under the same roof, you'd have a problem with Yolanda coming over and you know it."

"What's the baby doing?"

"I don't know, but I wish she'd stop." Blowing out another breath, "I'm really uncomfortable."

"You don't think you're in labor, do you?"

"No, I've had this pain before."

"When?"

"A few days ago, while I was in Los Angeles."

"And, you didn't think it important to say anything to me about it?"

"No, Ronnie, I didn't. Why would I? It's just part of the process. Besides, Dr. Anderson said it's normal."

"You're not scheduled to travel anymore before the baby is due, are you?"

Looking out the window, "next Wednesday."

"I don't want you to go."

Turning to face me, "what?"

"You heard me. I don't want you travelling by yourself."

"I'm not going to be by myself."

Raising my voice, "am I going to be with you?"

"No."

"Then you're going to be by yourself." Covering my mouth, "they need to conference call you or something."

Looking at me, "what was that?"

"They need to find another way to include you in on the meeting that doesn't require you having to travel."

"Whatever, Ronnie." Looking out the window again, "that's one of the reasons I don't want us living together."

"Because I'm looking out for you and my baby?"

"Because, you think you can tell me what to do."

I'm not arguing with her over this. She's not going. I'll just figure out a way to keep her home. "Why don't you ask Yolanda and her man to come to the house tonight and we can all hang out together?"

Head cocked to the side, she's looking at me, "are you serious? You can't stand Yolanda. Why would I invite her to your house for you to mistreat her?"

"You think I'd actually invite her into our home to mistreat her?"

"Hell, yeah!"

"I won't, I promise." Placing my hand on top of hers, "I want you to stay with me tonight. If she goes to your house, I won't see you until tomorrow."

"Okay. I'll ask her." Pointing at me with her other hand, "I'm serious, Ronnie, you better not mistreat her."

"I won't. I already said I wouldn't." Squeezing her hand, "you need to call her so she doesn't go to your place."

Arriving home, Michelle and I are in the kitchen preparing finger foods for *our* guests. "I'm glad you have food here."

"Why wouldn't I? You eat when you're here, so I have to."

"You don't have to be rude."

Here we go. "I'm not being rude."

"Yes, you are. Just remember, I'm only here because you asked. I have no problems going home."

Going into the refrigerator, "I'm not going to argue with you over nothing."

Hearing the doorbell ringing, "It's always nothing when it comes you. And, don't forget, be nice to my friend."

Following her to answer the door, "I said I'd be nice." Reaching around her to open the door, I put on the fakest smile I can muster for this skank and her man.

Rolling her eyes at me, she hugs her *friend* and then her friend's man. "I'm so glad you're finally here."

"Hello, Ronnie." Scrunching her face at me, "this is Daren." Smiling back at Michelle, "girl, I almost forgot how to get here."

Shaking Daren's hand, "hey man, come on in."

Leading everyone into the family room, Michelle and I bring in the food and drinks. After listening to Yolanda talk about absolutely nothing, I suggest to Daren that we go upstairs to watch some basketball.

Handing him a beer, "how long you been dating Yolanda?"

"Just a little over a year." Taking a swig from his beer, "congratulations on the baby."

"Thanks. I can't wait for her to get here."

"I'll bet. Michelle's a good person. I'm really glad she's Yolanda's friend."

"They've been friends since college."

"That's what Yolanda told me."

Daren isn't so bad. I actually like him. "They're like sisters. When we were in college, they were thick as thieves."

"I know. That's what she told me." Shaking his head, he laughs, "man, those two are a trip! They talk about everything."

Nodding my head, "that's the damned truth."

"Man, one night Yolanda suggested I try something that Michelle told her that y'all had done. I'm like, I'm not taking lessons on how to sex my woman from your best friend."

What the hell...I've never known Michelle to give details about our sex life. As a matter of fact, I once overheard Yolanda say that Michelle doesn't like to share details.

"That girl actually talked me into going down on her while she was spread out on my kitchen's island and then picking her up with her shit in my face."

What! I've never done anything like that before.

"Man, that shit turned me on big time. I wore her ass out that night." Laughing out loud, "I know men talk, but women, they give blow by blow details." Looking over at me, "you alright?"

Hell. The. Fuck. No. I'm not alright. I'm about to tell this motherfucker. Getting up from the sofa, "yeah. I'll be back."

Going downstairs, I swear, if this woman wasn't pregnant with my baby, I'd kill her ass. Going into the dining room, "Michelle. I need to talk to you for a minute."

Turning in my direction, "what's wrong?" Getting up from the table, she follows me into our bedroom.

What do I say to her? I'm mad as hell. I know I promised not to bring up the past, but this is some bullshit!

"Ronnie, what's wrong?"

"I want to ask you a question." Leaning against our bedroom door, she's sitting on the bed. "When did I spread you out on our island and eat you out?"

The look on her face is priceless. She looks like her eyes are going to pop out of her head. "What?"

"No what. When the hell did I do that?"

"Who told you about that?"

"Correct me if I'm wrong, but what I was told is that I had you laid out on the kitchen island while I ate you out and then," chuckling out loud, "picked you up with your *shit* in my face." Moving to squat down next to her, "then what did I do?"

Staring at me, "you know damn well it wasn't you who did that." Getting up from the bed, "have I ever asked you how you fucked some woman?"

"Don't reverse this shit."

"Ronnie, it happened. I can't change it. I can't even believe you would call me in here to even ask me about what happened with Malcolm. What can you do about it?"

Dropping my head, I whisper, "nothing." Getting up and sitting on the bed, I have my elbows on my knees with my face in my hands, "did you enjoy it?"

"You have really lost your mind." Coming to sit down next to me, "did you enjoy sleeping with Felecia? Cause according to her, the dick was all that." Placing her hand on the lower part of her stomach, "we weren't even married when it happened. You need to let it go."

"You're still friends with him."

"And?"

"Do you know how bad it hurts to know that another man touched you? It's my own fault, I know that, but it hurts all the same." Grabbing her other hand, "listen, I'm sorry." Staring at her, "it's just Daren was up there telling me how Yolanda wanted him to try something that we had done and I guess I flipped."

"Out! You flipped out."

"I want to be the only man to satisfy you. Only me."

"Ronnie, sex is different with someone you don't love. It's just physical. As good as it may be, you're left feeling empty when it's over." Lip turned up into a smile, "but when you love someone, the whole experience is amazing. Nothing else compares. It doesn't even come close."

"So, I'm better."

Getting up from the bed, she says over her shoulder, "you're crazier!"

"Crazy about you."

Chapter Forty Seven

Oh God, I can't get comfortable. We've had two false calls already, so I'm not trying to go to the hospital only to have them send us back home again.

Looking over at the clock, it's three in the morning and Ronnie is snoring too loud.

We finally agreed that I move in with him with the understanding that I keep my apartment. So far, things haven't been too bad with the exception of him trying to control me travelling for my job.

Okay, this hurts! Looking over at the clock again, "Ronnie, wake up. My contractions are ten minutes apart."

"You sure," he's asking in a groggy voice.

"Ah! Yes, I'm sure. They're ten minutes apart." Getting out of bed, "Ronnie! Get up, now!"

Jumping out of bed, "babe, I'm sorry." Grabbing his jeans, "what are you doing?"

"I'm taking a shower."

"What? You took a shower before you came to bed."

"I don't care. I have to be fresh."

Stopping dead in his tracks, he stares at me. Shaking his head, "hurry up."

Arriving to the hospital, I feel like I'm about to split in half. Damn, this hurts.

Getting out of the car, he runs around to the passenger side to open the door. Seeing the security guard approaching, "sir, I'll help her into a wheelchair while you park your car."

"Thanks." Running back to get into the car, "I'll be right back."

Waiting for Ronnie to return, the security guard is overly talkative. "This your first baby?"

Nodding my head.

"My girl just had a baby a few weeks ago."

"Congratulations."

"Thanks. I got three. Two boys and now a baby girl."

With my eyes closed, I nod again. What's taking Ronnie so long?

"My first baby mama is mad as hell that I have a new baby. I keep telling her that she number one."

Glancing up at him, "could you please be quiet?"

"My bad."

Finally, Ronnie is back. "What took you so long?"

"I was only gone like three minutes."

"Three minutes too long."

Making it to the maternity floor, everything seems to be happening too fast. "Ms. Barnett, we've called Dr. Anderson and he's on his way."

"Okay, thank you." I'm trying to do this without the epidural like Sharon suggested, but I don't know if I can.

Holding my hand, "you sure you want to do this without pain medication?"

"I'm going to try."

Michelle has been in labor for five hours now and I'm about to lose my mind. She's in so much pain and still, she's refusing the epidural.

"Okay, mom and dad, you're angel is ready to make her entrance into the world. "Dr. Anderson says, after examining Michelle.

After four pushes, Michelle collapses against the pillow. "Come on baby, we're almost there. Come on babe. We can do this."

"Ronnie, please stop talking to me." She says, through clenched teeth. "We're not pushing, I am."

"Okay, Michelle, one last push." Dr. Anderson says. "Come on. Put everything you've got into it."

Looking down, I see the top of my daughter's head. This is so amazing. Looking back at Michelle, I love this woman so much.

"Keep pushing mom, come on. One more push."

Watching Dr. Anderson pull my daughter out, he tells me to cut the umbilical cord. So full of emotion, I have tears streaming down my face. Hearing my daughter's cry, I am overcome with a joy I've never felt before. As they're laying my crying baby on Michelle's chest, I lean down and kiss her. "Thank you baby. This is the best gift you could ever give me."

Rubbing our daughter's back, she looks up at me, "thank you Ronnie, I love you."

The next few hours are a blur. I've called my parent's and Michelle's. Watched her breast feed, which was damn erotic, and now I'm sitting here holding my princess while her mother is sleeping. Looking down at her small body in my arms, I have to do right by her.

Squirming around, she lets out a wail. "Why are you crying princess? Are you hungry?"

"She sure has healthy lungs, doesn't she?"

"She's perfect." Standing, "I think my little princess is hungry?"

"Yeah, I think she is too." Holding out her arms, she positions Morgan like the nurse showed her and begins to nurse.

"Are you still in pain?"

Looking up at me, she frowns. "A little. Can you stop staring at me like that?"

Not attempting to move my eyes, "how am I staring at you?"

"I don't know. It's kind of perverted though."

Finally, I look up to meet her eyes, "I like watching you breastfeed is all. It's, I don't know. Hell, it turns me on."

"You're being nasty." Frowning at me, "how is watching a baby breastfeed sexy?"

Leaning down to kiss Morgan's little hand, "it just is. Will you let me taste your milk?"

"Hell no. Give me a blanket."

"Okay, I won't stare. Well, I'll try not to."

"You're staring now."

"Okay." Going to sit back down in the rocking chair beside the bed, "I can't believe she's finally here, seven days before Valentine's Day."

Looking down at the baby, I'm wondering what she's thinking. Judging by the expression on her face, it's something serious.

"Dr. Anderson said we could go home on Friday. I'm sure glad we finished her room when we did." Not responding, she's still staring down at our baby. "Our parents should be here later today." Still nothing. "What are you thinking?"

Glancing up at me, she looks back down at the baby. "My aunt Carolyn was right, I've never really taken a liking to kids. I don't know why, I just never have. I had never even held a baby until Rhonda had MJ."

"Are you worried about that?"

"No, I'm not worried." She says, rubbing Morgan's hand. "But, this tiny baby is expecting me to take care of her." Letting out a breath, "I don't want to let her down. There's a part of me that knows how to be selfish. I can't be like that with a baby."

Nodding my head, "know what I was thinking while you were asleep?"

"What were you thinking?"

Coming to stand beside the bed, "I have to do right by the both of you. You are the most important people in my life." Because I've stopped talking, she looks up at me. "Michelle, living together isn't enough." Moving to place the baby on her shoulder, "can I burp her?"

Passing the baby to me, "remember what you said. Don't go back on your word now."

Rubbing Morgan's back, I love this baby so much. "I know what I said. At the time, it was just the two of us. Having my little princess here changes things."

Before she can respond, our parents are here.

Chapter Forty Eight

"Hold on a second, Todd." Exhaling my breath. Today, Morgan is seriously trying my patience. Damn Ronnie. Because he holds her all the time, I can't get anything done unless she's in my arms.

"Sounds like your baby is upset, you can call me back."

I should have had this report in his hands two hours ago. Bouncing Morgan up and down, while patting her back to calm her down, "Todd, give me a few minutes and I'll email it to you."

"Alright, I'll call you back if I have any questions." Clearing his throat, "if it's okay with you?"

Rocking Morgan, I'm frowning, what the hell does he mean by that? "Of course, it's okay."

"I didn't mean it like that Michelle. After all, you are technically still on maternity leave."

"I know you didn't and I'm sorry for snapping like I did. Morgan is a lot of work."

"That's all babies. Believe me, my wife can probably share stories with you."

"Thank you, Todd. Give me a few minutes and you'll have the report."

Hanging up the phone, "look Morgan, you're going to have to give me a few minutes to work." Placing her in her bouncy, she starts crying even louder. Her noise, added to the ringing phone is so frustrating! "Hello!"

"Hey girl." Rhonda says, laughing into the phone, "sounds like Ms. Morgan is over there giving you the blues."

"Yeah, she is." Picking her up again, "she wants to be held all the time. I can't do anything without having her attached to me."

"I've told Ronnie over and over not to hold her so much. What you're going to have to do is let her cry. If she's not hungry and has a clean diaper, put her in a room and close the door. It's not going to kill her to cry."

Listening to Rhonda, it's the exact same thing that Linda told me to do. "I feel like I'm going to lose my mind sometimes with her. It's like she's the ideal baby when Ronnie is here. But with me, she's totally opposite."

"Her daddy has her spoiled." She responds. "Well, I'm not going to hold you long. I was calling to see if you wanted to get together with me and Sharon for mom's day out next weekend?"

Emailing the report to Todd, I get up to walk with Morgan. Bouncing her up and down to get her to sleep, "I guess so. Where are we going to meet?"

"I was thinking we could meet in Bakersfield."

"Free massages," we both say at the same time.

"We can leave the kids with the men. Hell, give Ronnie a taste of his own medicine."

Rolling my eyes, "how so?"

"Let him have to deal with Ms. Morgan all day."

Rolling my eyes again, "believe me, it wouldn't bother him in the least. All he'll do is sit in front of the television, holding her the entire time."

"Sharon mentioned Aiden doing the same thing with Maddison and we see how bad that heffa is."

Finally, she's asleep and I have a lot to do. Cutting the conversation short, "I'd like a day off. I'll talk to Ronnie when he gets home."

"Okay, let me know." Pausing, "you know Michelle, I'm really glad that you and Ronnie are back together. He has his ways, but he loves you and that baby."

Right now, I don't want to talk about Ronnie. He listens to nothing that I say concerning this baby. "I'll call you later."

Hanging up the phone, I'm heading into the bedroom to lay the baby down in her bassinette. Glancing over at the clock, it's almost five so he should be home soon.

Sitting down on the bed, I really want to go back to my place for a couple of hours, without Ronnie and without Morgan.

Looking down at my little angel, she looks so much like her dad. From her Asian eyes, to her button nose to her perfect lips. How can this beautiful baby be so much work?

Rhonda's right, he loves this little girl. Thinking back to Valentine's Day, she was only seven days old and got roses. I thought it was the sweetest thing and he was so happy. Laughing to myself as I get up to walk over to the dresser, he also gave me an engagement ring on that day.

Hearing the chime of the alarm, he's home.

Coming into the bedroom, "hey, babe. Morgan asleep?"

Walking past him, I'm going back into the office, "yes, and please don't wake her up."

Taking off his jacket and tie, "what's wrong with you?"

Looking back at him, "nothing, Ronnie. Nothing's wrong. Besides the fact that I didn't get anything done today, everything is great."

"What were you trying to get done?"

"Take a shower, work on some reports." Scowling at him, "does it matter?"

Going over to check on Morgan, "I'm home now. Do what you need to do. I've got the baby."

Michelle is always so damned moody. After talking to my mom earlier today, I realize that having a new baby, especially for someone who never had to take care of one before, is overwhelming.

My mom suggested that I always remember to give her a few minutes to herself while I take care of the baby. She also suggested that I stop holding my little princess so much, which is hard to do. She's so beautiful. Rubbing my finger across her chubby cheek, she's surely a blessing from God.

Going into the closet to change, I keep wondering if I could have possibly loved our first child as much as I love my baby girl. One things for sure, Michelle and I almost never talk about the first pregnancy. Outside of the guilt associated with the loss, it's probably for the best.

Walking past the office, I hear her on the phone talking to somebody. Hearing her laugh, something I haven't heard in a while, I stop to see if I can figure out who she's talking to.

"You're so silly! No, Ronnie's home. I wish. She's sweet, but she's a lot of work! No, I'm still breastfeeding. She's three months old. What's been up with you? Ronnie's off on Friday, maybe we can do lunch. Alright, Malcolm. Okay. Talk to you later."

Malcolm. She must be out of her damn mind if she thinks I'm going to let her go out with his ass.

I should... Nah, I'm not going to say anything, she's just not going.

Going back into our bedroom after grabbing a bottled water, I decide to make her a hot bath to help her relax. Then maybe, she'll give me some so that I can relax. She got cleared over a month ago by her doctor and still won't give me any because I insist on my baby being in the room with us. I still don't understand her point, it's not like she's in the bed with us.

"What are you doing?"

Sitting on the side of our garden tub, I look back over my shoulder, "making my other baby a nice, hot bath."

Coming to stand next to me, she puts her hand on my back, "that's sweet of you."

Standing, I place my hands at her hips, "I know you've had a rough day taking care of the baby so I thought a hot bath is just what you need to relax."

"Among other things," she says, barely audible.

Smirking at her, "it's not like I haven't been trying."

"No, it's just you want to do it with the baby in the room."

"She's a baby, she won't know what we're doing."

"How do you know?" Shaking her head, "I won't feel right doing that with her in the room." Pulling away from me, "and why is our sex limited to just the bedroom again?"

Damn! "The pregnant Michelle did decide to stick around, huh?"

Taking her shirt off, she throws it at me. "What do you mean by that?"

"The Michelle who likes sex and doesn't have a problem telling me."

Rolling her eyes, "answer my question."

Picking up her shirt, I'm watching her as she finishes getting undressed. Leaning against the bathroom counter, she looks good. The only sign of her having been pregnant are the curves. Her stomach is flat like before and that ass is on point. "If we're in another room, we may not hear her."

"What was the purpose of buying baby monitors if we're not going to use them?" She says, standing before me completely naked as she gets into the tub.

Staring at her, my dick is so damn hard I feel like it's about to burst through my sweats. Rubbing my hand down the front of my pants, "I like keeping her close."

Laying back in the tub with her eyes closed, "then you don't want any."

"How long are you going to hold out?"

Opening one eye, she smirks, "who says I'm holding out."

Standing up straight, "what the hell does that mean? You better be holding out because if I find out differently, we're going to have some serious problems."

Smiling with her eyes closed, she lifts her left leg up in the tub, "calm down. I'm only joking."

"You better be joking. Don't play like that, it's not funny." Picking up her pants and underwear from the floor, "enjoy your bath. And stop teasing me."

This bath is just what I needed. Talking to Malcolm today also helped. He just found out that his wife is pregnant and suggested that we all get together to celebrate. But since Ronnie knows about our little tryst, I'm not so sure that's a good idea.

Hearing Morgan start to cry, I move to get out of the tub so that I can feed her. At least she slept long enough for me to enjoy my bath.

Coming through the door holding the baby, "I think she's hungry."

"Probably so. Give me a few minutes." I'm saying as I'm reaching for a towel to cover myself.

Staring at me, his eyes are dark, "where are you going to feed her?"

"Upstairs."

Still staring at me, he slowly turns and walks out of the bathroom.

Yeah, let's see how long you last Mr. Wen.

Going upstairs to wait for Michelle, I'm seriously rethinking Morgan sleeping in the room with us. She's right. We have baby monitors all over the house.

Sitting down on the sofa, I have Morgan lying back in my lap with one hand resting behind her head and neck and the other underneath her bottom, "you know daddy loves you, right princess? I know you do. Well listen, daddy has needs." Smiling up at me, she's cooing. "See, you're a genius, I know you understand. Like I was saying, daddy has needs. Mommy's not going to take care of my needs if you're in the room with us." Squirming around, she has her fist in her mouth. "What daddy needs you to do is sleep through the night." Scrunching her face up, she lets out a whimper, "I know, it's a lot to ask of you princess. Okay, let's compromise, give me at least two hours and I'll stay up with you all night." Cooing at me, "thank you princess."

Walking into the room wearing black stretch pants and a cotton shirt with buttons in the front, "what are you thanking her for?"

Lifting Morgan up so that I can kiss her, "nothing much, right princess? We were just talking while waiting for you."

Taking the baby from me, she smells good. Sitting down, she positions Morgan so that she can nurse. Smiling down at her, she leans back into the sofa cushions. "By the way, Rhonda called earlier today to invite me to have a mother's day out next weekend in Bakersfield."

"Leaving me and Morgan here?" Seeing the look in her eyes, I recall my conversation with my mother, "I think it would be good for you to have some time to yourself. We'll be fine."

"Thank you."

Leaning down to kiss her on the lips, "you're welcome." Staring at her for a few more minutes, "I'm going to make us something for dinner."

Nodding her head, she rubs Morgan's hand with her pointing finger. Morgan in turn grabs Michelle's finger and holds it. "You are the sweetest little angel." Laughing to herself, "sometimes."

After dinner, sandwiches, we stay upstairs watching movies. Around nine thirty, I take Morgan from Michelle to get her to sleep. Telling me that she's going to check her emails, I take my baby into her room. Turning on the monitor, I head downstairs to the office. Looking up from the computer, she smiles.

"Morgan's asleep."

Looking at the clock on the computer, she nods.

Walking towards the desk, I have an idea. We haven't been together in a while, about two weeks prior to finding out about Malcolm's ass spreading her across his island to be exact. "You almost done working?"

Nodding her head, "almost." She says, in a frustrated sigh.

Pushing the chair back away from the desk, I pull her up. "Can you take a break?" Not giving her a chance to respond, I grab the back of her head, pulling her into a kiss while using my free hand to pull at the hem of her shirt. Breaking the kiss long enough to pull her shirt over her head, I recapture her lips. Hearing her moan into my mouth, I cup her butt, pulling her against my erection as I grind into her.

Reaching over to clear a space on the desk, I lay her back while pulling her stretch pants and underwear down at the same time. Leaning over her, I unclasp her bra as I suck her nipple into my mouth. Hearing her moan, "I've been wanting to taste your milk for a while now." Going to the other breast, I'm in heaven. Moving back up to kiss her lips, I begin to trail kisses down her body until I reach my desired destination. Pulling the chair to sit, I began to feast on her. "You taste so good, baby."

Squirming around on the desk, she has her head thrown back. "Ah, Ronnie. Hmm, don't stop!" Hearing her scream out for the second time, I'm going to wipe out all memories of that damn island shit from her brain. Using her heels to lift off the desk, I grab her butt and start using my tongue to penetrate her, she explodes.

Standing to remove my pants and boxers, I pull her onto my lap so that she's straddling me. Shifting so that I can enter her, she looks at me. "I've missed you."

"I've missed you too." Meeting me thrust for thrust, I'm trying hard not to cum.

"Where's Morgan?"

"In her room."

"Really?"

"Really."

"Raising her feet to rest on the chair, she starts to ride me. Riding me like she's never done before. "Ah damn baby, I'm going to cum!" Grabbing hold of her hips, we're banging the hell out of each other. Watching the expression on her face does something to me. Holding her in place, I'm pumping into her. Going still, I explode.

Trying to catch our breaths, neither one of us making an attempt to move. Finally, she raises up to look at me, "I take you decided that it's okay for Morgan to finally sleep in her room."

Smiling at her, "you weren't going to give me any otherwise." Helping her to get up, we're grabbing our clothes to go into our bedroom. Oh shit, "babe, please tell me that you've been taking your pills."

Looking over her shoulder, "a little late to be asking me that now, don't you think?"

"I have no problem with you giving me more babies."

"Well I do. So yes, I'm taking those damn things faithfully."

After taking a shower together, we're lying in bed with her head resting on my chest. "Babe, your lease is going to be up next month at your *apartment,* what are your plans?"

Rubbing her finger across my chest, "I'm not sure." Letting out a slow breath, "what do you think I should do?"

"You're asking me?"

Raising her head up, she looks at me, "yes, I'm asking you. What do you think I should do?"

Taking her left hand into mine, "I know what I'd like for you to do, but this has to be your decision."

"What would you," pointing her finger into my chest, "like for me to do?"

Creasing my brow, "well, you're the mother of my daughter, I love you with everything in me, I'd like for us to get married..." Looking into her eyes, "maybe you could not renew your lease and we make things official between us."

"I'll think about it."

Rolling her over on her back, "while you're thinking about it, I'm going to give you something else to think about."

Hearing Morgan's crying coming through the baby monitor, I glance over at the clock. It's after six, which means she slept through the night. Moving to get up, my body is aching.

Getting out of bed, I grab my robe and head upstairs. Picking Morgan up, I move to sit in the rocking chair and begin to nurse her. "I can't believe you slept all night."

Closing my eyes to clear my mind, I'm not sure what I should do about my lease. Maneuvering Morgan to my right breast, I move to rub my hand over her head. Glancing down at my hand, the engagement ring that Ronnie gave me on Valentine's Day is on my left ring finger.

"Morning babe." Ronnie says, coming into the room wearing his pajama bottoms with no shirt, rubbing his hand down the back of his neck. "I planned on getting up before you."

"It's okay. You have to work today."

"I took the day off."

"Good, I need some sleep." Lowering my head, "somebody in this room kept me awake last night and it wasn't Morgan."

"Are you complaining?"

"No. I'm definitely not complaining."

Coming to sit on the floor next to the rocking chair, "when she's done nursing, I can burp her."

"Know what I noticed this morning?"

Bringing his eyes up to meet mine, "what did you notice?"

Holding up my left hand, "that someone put this beautiful ring on my finger."

"Wonder who did that?"

"I don't know, but I don't think it was Morgan."

"I don't know, she's pretty intelligent."

"As smart as she is, I don't think she's mastered walking yet."

Looking at my hand, "wonder what the person who put that ring on your finger is trying to ask you?"

Raising my brows, "I don't know. Maybe somebody in this room can enlighten me?"

Grabbing my hand, "this is a nice ring." Rubbing his chin, "it appears to be a really expensive engagement ring." Looking up at me, "which means that *whomever* put this ring on your finger is trying to ask you to marry him because he loves you."

"Sounds like a good man."

"He's only good because he realized that the woman he loves is a jewel." Dropping his head, "he almost lost her. Thank God he learned his lesson."

"What lesson was that?"

"When she decided to love herself more, she changed."

"How so?"

"She made him learn that he couldn't half step." Looking at me, "it's all or nothing and I'm giving her my all."

Epilogue

"Sean. Man, you leaving?"

Leaning against my car, I look back to see Sebastian walking in my direction, "nah, I just needed a break from y'all."

Opening the door to his truck, "I hear you." He says, laughing. "I'm not going to lie, we love being with your family." Walking back towards the house, "there's never a dull moment."

"Tell me about it."

My sister, Rhonda, her husband, Michael, along with their three children, Michael Jr., Andrew and Taylor, have just purchased a new home here in Bakersfield. And like with every other occasion, they decided to have a family gathering to celebrate.

It wouldn't be so bad if I didn't have to deal with watching my brother, Ronnie, and his wife, Michelle, constantly flirting back and forth with each other. Or, listening to their thirteen month old daughter, Morgan, constantly screaming at the top of her lungs, "*stop! My daddy! My mommy! Mine! No!*" Those are the only words she seems to know and those few words have grated on my last damn nerve today.

Then there's my sister, Sharon, and her husband, Aiden. They are living proof that people should be licensed to have kids. For some reason, God saw fit to bless them with twins. Their son, Jaxson, really isn't that bad. It's his spoiled ass sister, Maddison, who needs a serious ass whipping. I still can't believe that for the past hour or so, this three year old little girl has been literally terrorizing her cousins and not one adult, especially her parents, have said anything. Yeah, she needs her ass whipped.

Also here with us is our family friend, Sebastian, and his very pregnant wife, Camille, along with their four year old son, Sebastian Jr. Scratching my forehead, I think I might actually like SJ. When he thought no one was watching, he knocked the hell out of Maddison and moved on like nothing happened.

And last but not least, are my parents. They're in hog heaven now that they have a house full of grandchildren that they can spoil.

After listening to my dad go on and on about me settling down and starting my own family, a given conversation when we're all together, I had to make an escape. Thus, my reasoning for being out here in this hot ass sun.

Feeling my phone vibrating in my pocket, it's my new business partner, Simone Edwards.

I was just fine working alone as the top pharmaceutical representative for Bio Heal Diagnostics until the powers that be decided that I needed a partner. Why they couldn't pair me up with Jonathan, I'll never know.

"Yeah."

"Yeah? Is that how you answer your phone?"

"It's Saturday, what do you want?"

Mumbling something under her breath, "I was calling to see if we could talk more about our little situation before Monday."

"There's nothing to talk about. You need to know your place and we'll get along fine."

Hesitating, "know my place? I'm just trying to come up with a way for us to amicably work together." Dramatically sighing, "Sean, how was I to know that I would be working with the guy who I had sex with on last Friday?"

"Whatever. You had to have known who I was. You're not stupid Simone, I know you did your homework before accepting that position."

"No, Sean. I'm not stupid and yes, I did do my homework. However, I don't recall us exchanging last names that night. As a matter of fact, we didn't do much talking at all. And for your information, I was just as surprised when Mr. Fields introduced us on Wednesday as you were."

"Yeah, right. You expect me to believe that?"

"Honestly, I don't care what you believe. I was only calling to see what we can do to establish a better work relationship. But, I see you're going to be a big baby about this whole situation. It was sex. It's not that big of a deal."

No big deal? Is this girl crazy? "I'm not being a baby. However, I don't like being screwed over and judging by what you just said, that's exactly what you tried to do."

"If I recall correctly, I wasn't the only one doing the screwing that night." Laughing into the phone, "oh, I get it."

"Get what?"

"You're used to being the one doing the loving and leaving. Is that it?"

"Go to hell Simone. Like I said, know your place and we should get along just fine."

Ending the call. I'm still pissed at my bosses for their decision to hire her. I've been the top sales representative in my division for two years in a row. Now that we've gone global, the company feels that Simone is going to be an asset because of her *vast* experience.

Who gives a damn about her vast experience? I sure as hell don't! I don't care that she's beautiful, smart and has the body of a goddess. I don't want to work with her. Especially, now that I've slept with her. I don't need her help to succeed in the global arena. I'm the man, I've been the man and I'm going to be the man.

Looking back towards the house, who am I kidding? Truth be told, I can't get last Friday out of my mind. I've been with plenty of women and not one of them compares e to Simone. She's right, I do like to love and leave their asses. I was actually thinking about keeping her around for a bit though. Now, I'm pissed and horny as hell and it's all because of her deceitful ass. Shaking my head, enough about her. I can't go out like my brother, Aiden and Sebastian – I'm going to *guard my heart*. The last thing I'm going to do is fall for some high maintenance chick who likes to play games. That is not going to happen. Point blank, she needs to know her place.

I hope you enjoyed this book. Please share your thoughts by emailing me at dcwilliams3love@gmail.com

www.ingramcontent.com/pod-product-compliance
Lightning Source LLC
Chambersburg PA
CBHW030623130626
46552CB00002B/686